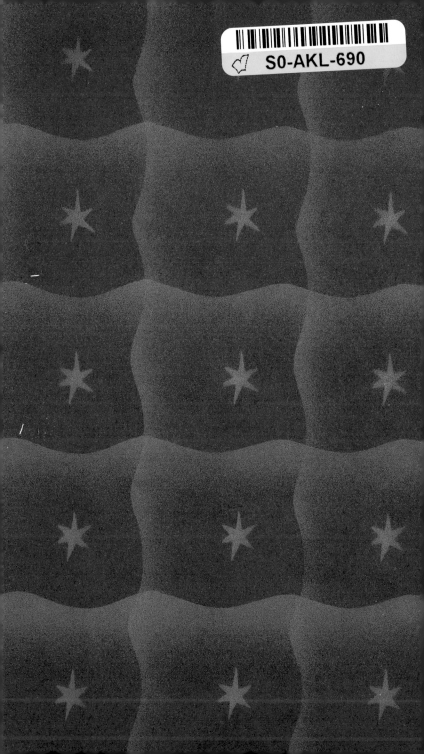

LYND
WARD

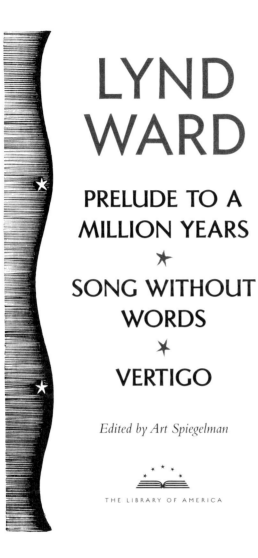

LYND
WARD

PRELUDE TO A
MILLION YEARS

★

SONG WITHOUT
WORDS

★

VERTIGO

Edited by Art Spiegelman

THE LIBRARY OF AMERICA

www.loa.org

The paper used in this publication
meets the minimum requirements of the American
National Standard for Information Sciences–
Permanence of Paper for Printed Library Materials,
ANSI Z39.48–1984.

The endpapers are adapted from a design created by
Lynd Ward for the binding boards of *Prelude to a Million Years*
(New York: Equinox Cooperative Press, 1933).

Distributed to the trade in the United States
by Penguin Group (USA) Inc.
and in Canada by Penguin Group Canada Ltd.

Library of Congress Control Number: 2010924274
ISBN: 978-1-59853-081-0

First Printing
The Library of America—211

MANUFACTURED IN THE UNITED STATES OF AMERICA

Lynd Ward: Prelude to a Million Years,
Song Without Words, Vertigo
is published with a gift in honor of

MARJORIE J. BERKLEY

CONTENTS

READING PICTURES

A FEW THOUSAND WORDS ON SIX BOOKS WITHOUT ANY

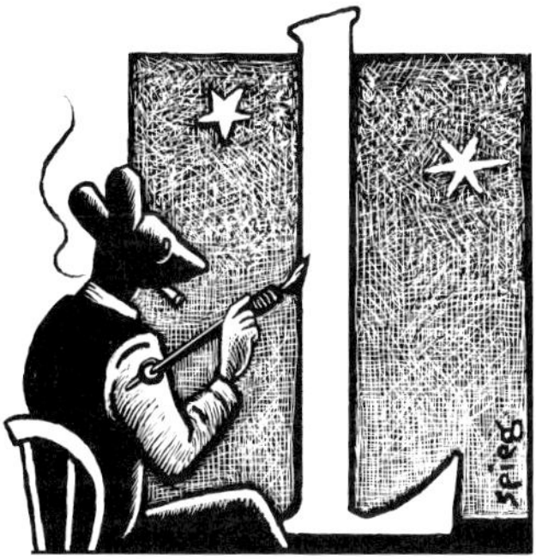

LYND WARD MADE BOOKS. He had an abiding reverence for the book as an object. He understood its anatomy, respected every aspect of its production, intimately knew its history, and loved its potential to engage with an audience. This is one of the reasons he commands our attention now, when the book as an object seems under siege.

He was born into a devout Methodist family in Chicago, in 1905. His father, Harry Frederick Ward, a progressive minister, imbued him with the social conscience and activism, as well as the pronounced Protestant work ethic, that informed his work and life. (In 1920 his father became the first chairman of the ACLU, and in the 1950s he was blacklisted for his prominence in the Popular Front.) As a tubercular child, Lynd Ward pored over Gustave Doré's nineteenth-century Bible illustrations since his father forbade anything as profane as the Sunday funnies in their home. Denied a comic-strip vocabulary, Ward would grow up to help define a whole other syntax for visual storytelling.

Right after graduating from the Teachers College of Columbia University, Ward took off for a year of advanced study in Europe with his new bride, future author May McNeer. Fortunately for those who cherish his lifework, they ended up in Weimar Germany rather than in Paris. Instead of pursuing the formalist Modernism in the air on the Left Bank, he entered the Cabinet of Dr. Caligari, became steeped in German Expressionist art, and learned wood engraving from a German master.

Ward happened onto a copy of *Die Sonne*, an antic, free-associative story of a modern Icarus told in a book of sixty-three woodcuts by Frans Masereel. Exuberantly whacking into wood in high expressionist mode, the Flemish artist invented the woodcut novel, inspired Ward, and continues to inspire artists today, myself gratefully included. First published in a popular edition the year before Ward got to Germany, *Die Sonne* (the third of more than fifty such works made by Masereel over his lifetime) had an introduction by Carl Georg Heise, a champion of what came to be known a decade later as "Degenerate Art." Knowing only rudimentary German as a student in Leipzig, Ward couldn't have understood the introduction but must have savored Masereel's power to communicate past national and linguistic barriers.

Communication was central to Ward's developing aesthetic. In a 1949 essay for *The Horn Book*, looking back on the evolution of the book artist over the past twenty-five years, he noted that

> the book artist's fundamental problem involved a greater emphasis on art as communication. Curiously enough, this took place at a time when the field of painting gave rise to overriding tendencies towards abstract and esoteric expression. . . . It may very well be that what we see here is the separation of two elements that have always been present in the visual arts—the concern with communication and the concern with visual qualities that just "are," and are their own justification for being. In the minds of many . . . the present trend towards concern with formal qualities is inevitable and desirable. On the other hand, it can be contended that a balance between formal qualities in visual expression and concern with having something to say has resulted in some of the greatest visual statements of the past—Hogarth, Blake, Daumier, Goya, Callot, to name a few. . . .

In 1929, after Ward returned to New York and became a struggling freelance illustrator, he discovered *Destiny*, a German wordless novel by Otto Nückel. Nückel's sole work in the form followed Masereel's example, but with a more cinematic narrative flow, presenting a highly coherent, vehemently melodramatic tale of a prostitute's life and death in luminous and painterly lead engravings. *Destiny* struck the twenty-four-year-old Ward hard, galvanizing him to produce the 139 narrative wood engravings that became *Gods' Man* later that same year. It was an immediate success. (Released in October

1929, in the same week as the stock-market crash that ushered in the Great Depression, it went on to sell over twenty thousand copies in the next four years.) *Gods' Man* introduced the woodcut novel and Lynd Ward to America and still remains the most emblematic and popular of his six published books in this genre.[*]

Gods' Man is also emblematic in an almost medieval sense, with its stark symbolism and its black-and-white depictions of good and evil on a Faustian theme. Our Hero, a destitute artist seeking fame and fortune, accepts a magic brush from a Mysterious Stranger. His rapid rise proves hollow, but he flees the corrupt City, meets a beautiful goatherd, and lives a life of Edenic beatitude until the Mysterious Stranger comes to collect payment and Our Hero dies. Despite the polytheistic implications of the oddly positioned apostrophe in its title, *Gods' Man* is a cautionary tale about the Sin of Pride.

The visual style of this first book, inflected by the Moderne streamlining of Rockwell Kent as well as by the Expressionist films of Murnau and Lang—veers away from the gestural Modernism that informs Masereel and Nückel but looks back instead to medieval book artists and to classical woodcut masters from Albrecht Dürer to Thomas Bewick, a symptom of Ward's temperamental predisposition toward craftsmanship.

Filled with the earnest *Sturm und Drang* of a very young man, Ward's first novel had enough of an impact on Susan

---

[*] Three of the books discussed in this essay appear in a companion volume in the Library of America series, *Lynd Ward: Gods' Man, Madman's Drum, Wild Pilgrimage.*

Sontag thirty-five years later to make her shortlist of canonical "Camp" works in her influential "Notes on Camp." It's a dubious distinction, although her essay does include the admonition that "Not only is Camp not necessarily bad art, but some art which can be approached as Camp (example: the major films of Louis Feuillade) merits the most serious admiration and study." Some of Ward's images are unintentionally risible (the depiction of Our Hero idyllically skipping through the glen with the Wife and their child makes me snicker), but others (the two plates of Our Hero in the desolate canyons of the City after fleeing from the Mistress come to mind) are indelible, demonstrating his formidable powers of graphic composition.

 Ward's skill at miming expression and body language was impressive, but it was Ward's audacity and confidence in wrestling with a new *narrative* language that won my serious admiration as a young cartoonist. The genre of visual storytelling that Ward pioneered had even more severe constraints than the flexible languages already in place for cinema and comics. Rarely was silent film—a direct catalyst for the wordless book—ever as resolutely mute as the woodcut novel: intertitles and musical accompaniment helped transmit its meanings. The sign language of cartooning (motion lines, pain-stars, "emoticons" *avant la lettre*) seems more supple than illustration's language of visual symbol. The proof lay in one of the most felicitous spin-offs of Ward's success: a delirious parody of Ward's work and of silent-movie melodramas, *He Done Her Wrong*, by the comics genius Milt Gross. (I found a mass-market paperback of Gross's classic at fifteen, only seeing and relishing Ward's work four years later—as with much of my cultural education, I absorbed the parody before discovering the original.) Gross's book, a singular masterpiece first published in 1930, was subtitled "THE GREAT AMERICAN NOVEL and not a word in it—no music too." Maybe the limitations of drawn pantomime lend themselves more readily to comic effect than to tragedy.

Hoping to deepen the possibilities of his chosen idiom, Ward embarked on a more challenging second wordless novel: *Madman's Drum*, a book of 118 plates published a year after his first. Unlike the protagonist of *Gods' Man*, the artist was hardly undone by his ambition, but as he wrote in his 1974 collection, *Storyteller Without Words*:

> I realized, not without pain, that when I was work-
> ing on *Gods' Man* . . . I had probably seen things
> in too simple terms . . . inventing characters just
> to make a needed point, using them without suf-
> ficient consideration for their identities as persons
> with individual backgrounds, histories, and needs.
> . . . [T]here seemed an obvious need for a more
> sophisticated relation to the world and more in-
> evitability in the encounters between characters.
> It was possible, of course, that seeking this further
> dimension for characters whose impact is purely
> visual was asking for more than the medium could
> convey . . .

Ward went on to say: "One thing that impressed itself

on me as this second book gradually took shape was that
…working with a narrative sequence is, in more ways than
one, working in the dark." A few sections into *Madman's
Drum* the reader is likely to get lost in Ward's darkness.

The first pages are promising enough, introducing
what turns out to be the protagonist's father, a prosperous
and brutal seafaring slave trader; but then the storytelling slides into murky waters and begins to drown in its
own avowed desire to flesh out the stock character types
with individuated trajectories and tragedies. I swore to
honor Ward's intention to keep his narratives available to
each reader's subjective interpretation—uncontaminated
by nailing it to a cross of explanatory language—so I'll
only tell you (with the pride of one who has just won a
high-stakes game of charades) that the characters come
to a Bad End and the Sins of the Father are Visited unto
the Children. A couple of hints, should you decide to
read past this colon: the relatively large cast includes the
protagonist's two daughters who bear a narratively un-
fortunate physiognomic resemblance to their mother,
and occasionally new characters seem to sneak into the
story without quite being spotlighted.

Even the artwork is sometimes betrayed by its ambitions.
The very finely engraved lines and the rich palette of
hatched tones and patterns are sometimes harder to read
than the bold images in the first book, though Ward's
approach to pictorial composition only gets stronger. The
book has other virtues as well, not the least of which is its
well-told subplot about the daughter's communist lover

who is unjustly tried and hanged. Ward's keen sense of social justice—including his anger about the 1927 execution of Sacco and Vanzetti—is expressed more lucidly here than in the Sinful City sections of *Gods' Man*.

I've gone on at length about the book's failings because there is so much Ward learned from them. And my struggle to decipher his narrative clarifies for me the secret locked inside all wordless novels: the process of flipping pages back and forth, hunting for salient details and labeling them, shakes the words loose to yield meaning. Wordless novels are *filled* with language, it just resides in the reader's head rather than on the page.

Two years later Ward rebounded from his sophomore slump with a third woodcut novel that mastered the hard lessons learned: a narrative suite of 108 images called *Wild Pilgrimage.* Turning away from the novelistic complications of *Madman's Drum*, he produces a narratively and visually streamlined work that follows a single character, alternating between sequences of a mostly grim real world and the character's inner life. Ward returns to his first book's contrasts between corrupt civilization and pastoral nature, but now with sure-handed sophistication. Cynics may choose to sneer at its fervor or at the unnaturally fetishized figures and landscape that fall somewhere between Thomas Hart Benton and Tom of Finland, but its passion and even its odd sexual subcurrents are among its strengths.

The artist transcends the Black and White essence of his

form by embracing it—while innovatively substituting sanguine for black in the sequences of subjective reverie—and he finds a larger chromatic world than his work had yet achieved. *Wild Pilgrimage* is a proletarian novel and a psychological novel at the same time. It creates a lyrical visual poetry by weaving between a cascade of binaries: the Individual vs. Society, Freedom vs. Responsibility, Eros vs. Thanatos, Eden vs. Hades, the Subjective vs. the Objective, the Tree Trunk vs. the Smokestack, Angles vs. Curves. The symbols are at last rich in their allusive possibilities, able to evoke contradictory meanings: those trees that dominate the landscape shift from bearers of fruit to bearers of Billie Holiday's tragic Strange Fruit. In his dream-life our protagonist rescues humanity from the soul-crushing demon by decapitating it, and the head he holds up is his own!

The velocity of the narrative flow allows the book to achieve the artist's goal of inviting multiple readings. Steadily focused on the central character's movements through space—whether inner or outer—the book finds an easy rhythm of sequencing through time; unlike *Madman's Drum*, the fluidity of the storytelling keeps one's subvocal translating of images into words down to a soft murmur. More effectively than in *God's Man*, Ward's newly honed skills allow one to race forward through the book. He offers varied compositions, moods, and textured detail in the sumptuous deco plates, incorporating American Regionalism as well as a Futurist faceting of forms into a vocabulary that encourages the eye to linger and reread. *Wild Pilgrimage* is an effective work, in some ways the most accessible and satisfying of his books.

✳

Although most widely known for his woodcut novels, Lynd Ward, always a disciplined worker, became a prolific illustrator of limited-edition and trade books. He also designed and illustrated many children's books as that category began to blossom (and, in 1953, earned the Caldecott Medal for the gouache drawings he created for his picture book *The Biggest Bear*). Over the years he often proselytized in print for the glories of the integrally designed book. In the worst years of the Great Depression he even founded a progressive cooperative press, Equinox, devoted to artfully made literary and political books. In our digital future it's possible that *only* books of the sort Ward championed—aware of themselves as works of art, sensitive to the mechanical means needed to make them—will be left standing in the age of electronic reproduction.

I've long prized one of the sixteen books Equinox produced during its seven-year existence: a 1935 young-adult biography of John Reed, *One of Us*, with text by the literary editor of *New Masses*, Granville Hicks, and accompanied by thirty full-page lithographs by Ward; but I'd gladly trade it for his fourth woodcut narrative, *Prelude to a Million Years*, published by Equinox in 1933. Exquisitely made—hand-bound with a gold foil spine, its thirty plates printed directly from the woodblocks in Frenchfold signatures—the edition of 920 modestly priced signed copies quietly demonstrated Equinox's formal ideals while despairing of the world it was born into.

More a short musical prelude without words than a novel, *Prelude to a Million Years* revisits, with sharper eye and burin, *Gods' Man*'s theme of the artist trapped in a damned civilization. A sculptor, leaving his tenement atelier, encounters—in rapid succession—a mugger, a violent labor demonstration (the image of protestors being clubbed by police recurred in Ward's 1930s picture stories almost as frequently as it did in the rest of America), an almost equally violent display of jingoistic nationalism, and a drunk and dissipated woman (a prostitute and/or his ex-sweetheart) sprawled naked on her bed. He flees back to his studio in anguish, just in time for it and him to go up in flames. Welcome to a million years!

Another small-scale work with large-sized themes, *Song Without Words*, was published in an edition of 1,250 copies a few months after the Spanish Civil War began in 1936. A year earlier, Ward had become a founding member of the American Artists' Congress, organized to take "collective action against war and fascism." This *Song Without Words* is closer to a howl of pained outrage. It asks, as we still must, "How dare one bring a child into this sorry world?" Even those who may share my aversion to the Large-eyed Waif school of art must grant the prescience of showing the starving children trapped behind barbed wire under a swastika. Ward was a clear-headed visionary, a serious man of his time who foresaw the coming cataclysms.

The lone pregnant woman who wanders through the twenty-one rat- and vulture-infested plates raises her arms defiantly against the forces of evil as portrayed—it's one of the most intense and heartfelt anti-war images of the century!—in the form of an enormous skull with a tombstone city for teeth and death merchants peering from within its sockets, right before she gives birth. The song tries its damnedest to end on a hopeful note, as the woman and her mate sit naked before the radiant lights of the city, facing right, looking determinedly off the page, bracing for the future.

Ward's last complete woodcut novel, *Vertigo*, published in 1937, was well underway when he did *Song Without Words*. Genuinely novelistic in scope, it is a difficult work that grapples with perilously difficult times. As emblematic as Steinbeck's *Grapes of Wrath*, as ambitiously experimental as Dos Passos's *U.S.A.* trilogy, as apocalyptic as Nathanael West's *Day of the Locust*, it is a key work of Depression-era literature, and useful in understanding what is being done to us right now. Ward has moved past *Wild Pilgrimage*'s elegantly won game of checkers played with red and black markers, to engage in three-dimensional chess.

    The work is divided into three intertwined sections titled "The Girl," "An Elderly Gentleman," and "The Boy." After an introductory sequence, each of the sections is subdivided: the Girl's chapters are labeled by years (from 1929, the year of the Crash, to 1935); the Elderly Gentleman's twelve chapters are designated by months; the Boy's are specified by the days of the week. The search for connections between each section leaves one with a narrative of lives and dreams smashed by what Ward, in his 1974 reflections on the work, called "the obvious effect that vast, complicated, and impersonal social forces were having on the substance of so many individual lives."

A few key moments (an interesting word for images!) bind the Boy and the Girl, separated by those "impersonal social forces," to the life of the Elderly Gentleman, the head of the Eagle Corporation of America, that is depicted in the central section—the fulcrum—of the work. I am desperately trying to not give too much away, since *Vertigo* repays the concerted scrutiny it demands with interest; there's great pleasure and even emotional yield in uncovering the clues embedded as details within the pictures. Motifs, symbols, and contrasting situations weave the three parts into a merciless whole.

Complex in structure (rather than simply complicated, like *Madman's Drum*), *Vertigo* successfully takes up that earlier work's struggle to imbue archetypal characters with textured personhood. The genius of the work comes in Ward's sympathetic portrayal of the lonely, self-absorbed Elderly Gentleman, who emptily staves off the relentless passing of time while unmindfully sucking the lives out of all us Boys and Girls. The artist understood that

> it was obvious that apart from the symbolic figure wearing a label that a cartoonist uses by way of personification, it is impossible to establish a satisfactory single image that will convey the essence of what we mean by "impersonal social force." At the same time it is difficult for a reader to feel very

> much identification with a crowd; it is with a sin-
> gle human being, whether victim or hero, that we
> become emotionally involved. . . . It might even be
> possible to suggest that an impersonal social force
> is the accumulation of individual actions for which
> individuals are finally responsible.

The horrific enormous skull that looms over *Song Without Words* lurks right behind the Elderly Gentleman's culture, philanthropy, and melancholy, just as it continues to sit behind the smiling faces of the bankers, brokers, and other merchants of death today who individually might seem quite affable as dinner companions. Profoundly, the more sympathy mustered for the poor old rich gent, the more aware we become that the soul-crushing demon's head we hold up is our own!

It is a disservice to reduce *Vertigo* to its descriptions; it makes its humane qualities coarser. But the loving image of the unclothed Girl stretching unselfconsciously in all her glory at the beginning of her 1929 chapter, the con-trasting image of the pot-bellied naked Elderly Gentle-man standing forlorn at his mirror in the first image of his January chapter, and the jolting, stomach-wrenching last roller-coaster image that plummets us into the abyss of today's headlines, achieve a pathos far from the "campy" pleasures of *Gods' Man*. Welcome to a Million Years.

⁎

It seems natural now to think of Lynd Ward as one of America's most distinguished and accomplished graphic novelists. He is, in fact, one of only a small handful of artists anywhere who ever made a "graphic novel" until the day before yesterday. The ungainly neologism seems to have stuck since Will Eisner, creator of the voraciously inventive *Spirit* comic book of the 1940s, first used it on the cover of his 1978 collection of comics stories for adults, *A Contract With God*. It was a way to distance himself from the popular prejudices against the medium, and he often cited Ward's 1930s woodcut novels as an inspiration for his work and for the euphemism. But Ward's roots were not in comics, though his work is part of the same large family tree, belonging somewhere among the less worm-ridden branches of printmaking and illustration.

In the spring of 1970 I briefly met Lynd Ward in Binghamton, New York, at a small gallery show of his prints. I was a twenty-two-year-old cartoonist, a former student at nearby Harpur College, and, as I recall, I was by far the youngest and scruffiest person at the opening. I told him how much I admired his woodcut novels and he expressed surprise that I even knew the books. I asked what newspaper comics had been important to him and he explained that he hadn't been allowed to read them as a child. When pressed, he voiced appreciation for Hal Foster's *Prince Valiant*, which he discovered as an adult. I didn't share his enthusiasm—I thought Foster's work, with its captions positioned safely beneath each of the stately illustrations on his Sunday pages, was barely comics at all— but we went on to find common ground in our mutual esteem for the great old Socialist cartoonist Art Young before he turned back to talking to his grown-up friends.

Ward's wordless woodcut novels (like *Prince Valiant*, come to think of it) were easier for Western culture to embrace than comics in all their raffish splendor. In a pervasively influential eighteenth-century essay, *Laocoön: or The Limits of Poetry and Painting*, the German aesthetician Gotthold Lessing admonished Western culture against confusing the nature of poetry or prose—written forms whose province is time—with the nature of visual forms like painting and sculpture, whose province is spatial. Nothing could violate this long-held aesthetic taboo more directly than comics, a kind of picture-writing—the very *layout* of a comics artist's page insists on pulling the reader from one drawing to the next. Ward also trafficked in time, of course, but by inviting the eye to rest on each isolated composition—unsullied by written language—he was sneakier about it. To make a wood engraving is to insist on the *gravitas* of an image. Every line is fought for, patiently, sometimes bloodily. It slows the viewer down. Knowing that the work is deeply inscribed gives an image weight and depth.

Two years after meeting Lynd Ward, when I was beginning to seriously explore the limits and possibilities of comics, I drew a four-page comics story about my mother's suicide called "Prisoner on the Hell Planet." (It was eventually included in my long comic book for grown-ups that needed a bookmark, *Maus*.) I was then twenty-four years old (the same age as Ward when he made *Gods' Man*) and the scratchboard drawings I did were very influenced by Ward's engravings and by German Expressionist woodcuts.

When walking through that Binghamton gallery show back in 1970, I regretted that no original prints from Ward's woodcut novels were part of the exhibit, but I remember slowing down to notice that a number of the prints on display depicted trees and forests. I thought about the poetry of patiently carving into a dead tree to make a print on paper that commemorated the once-living thing. One beautifully structured print stayed with me (I later found it again, reproduced in *Storyteller Without Words*): a panoramic treescape of a young man in shadows, groping and climbing through the dense neuronal wickerwork of dappled trunks and branches, carefully exploring and working his way through the maze of marks that surround him. I've recently been told that it was intended to be a picture of the nature writer John Burroughs, but I'd thought of it as a moving self-portrait of the artist embedded in the wood, seeking slivers of light in the darkness and carving out a new medium. The print was called "Pathfinder."

> —*art spiegelman, nyc.*
> *April 2010*

PRELUDE
TO A MILLION YEARS

PRELUDE
TO A MILLION YEARS

A BOOK OF WOOD
ENGRAVINGS
BY LYND WARD

EQUINOX · NEW YORK · 1933

E

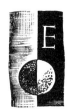

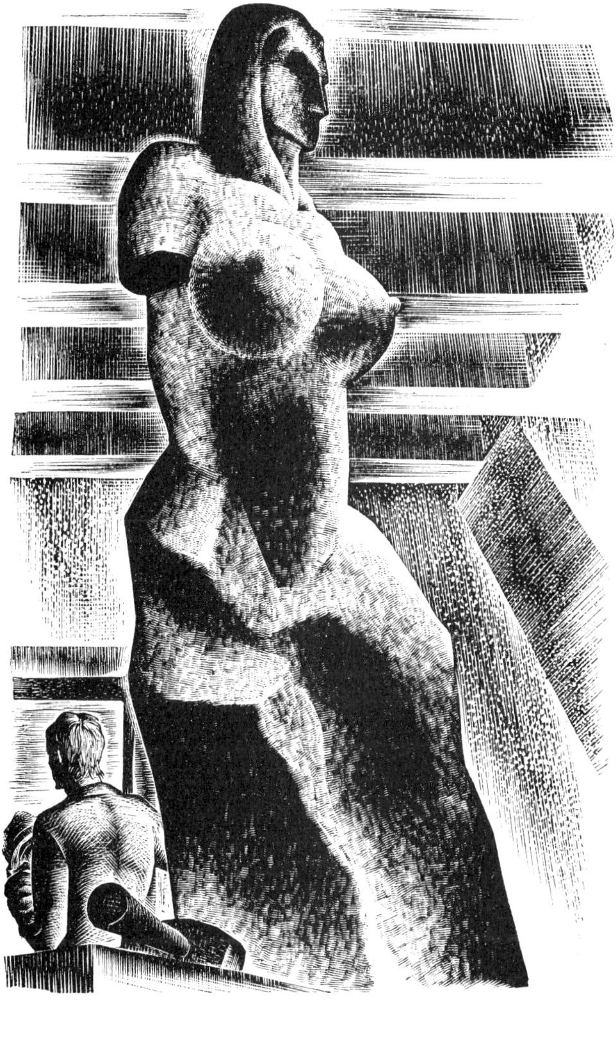

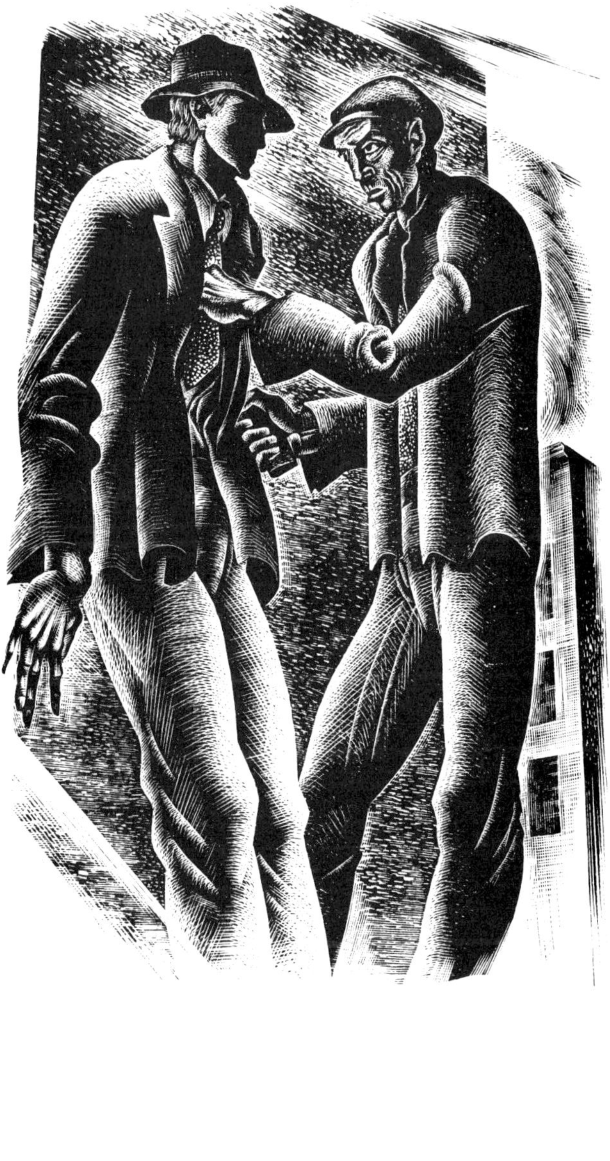

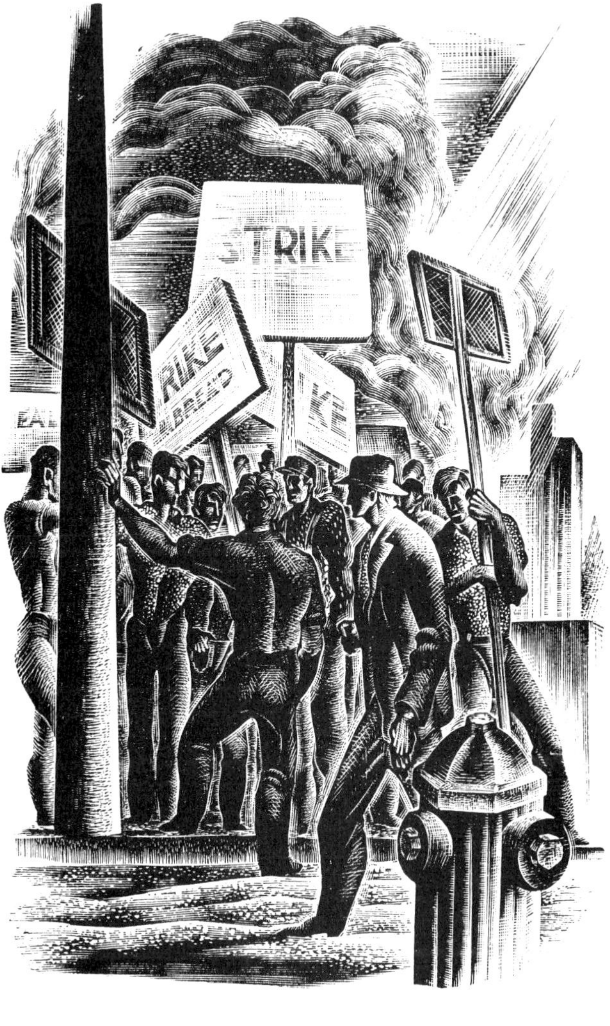
STRIKE
RIKE
KE

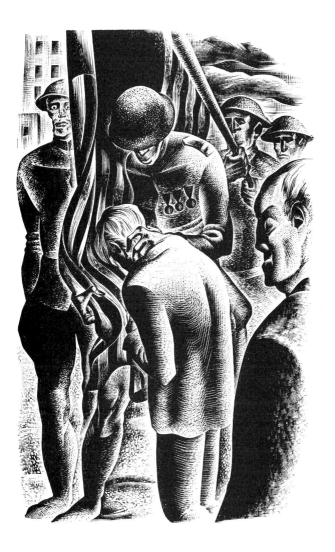

SONG WITHOUT WORDS

PUBLISHED IN NEW YORK BY

RANDOM HOUSE · INC · 1936

SONG

A BOOK OF ENGRAVINGS

WITHOUT

ON WOOD BY LYND WARD

WORDS

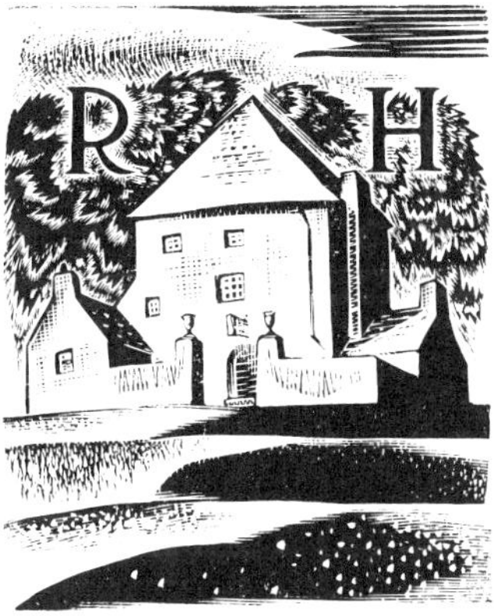
R H

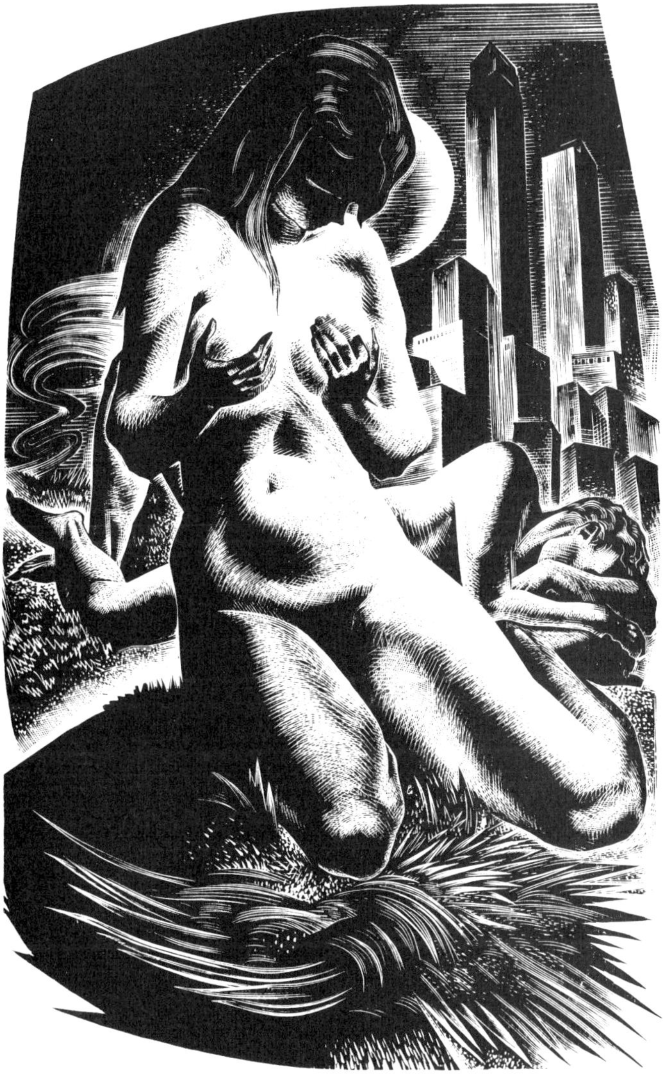

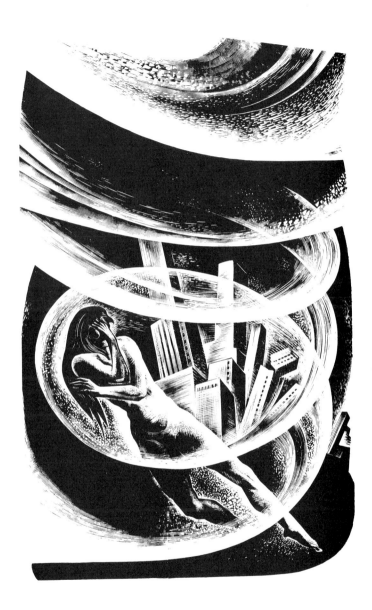

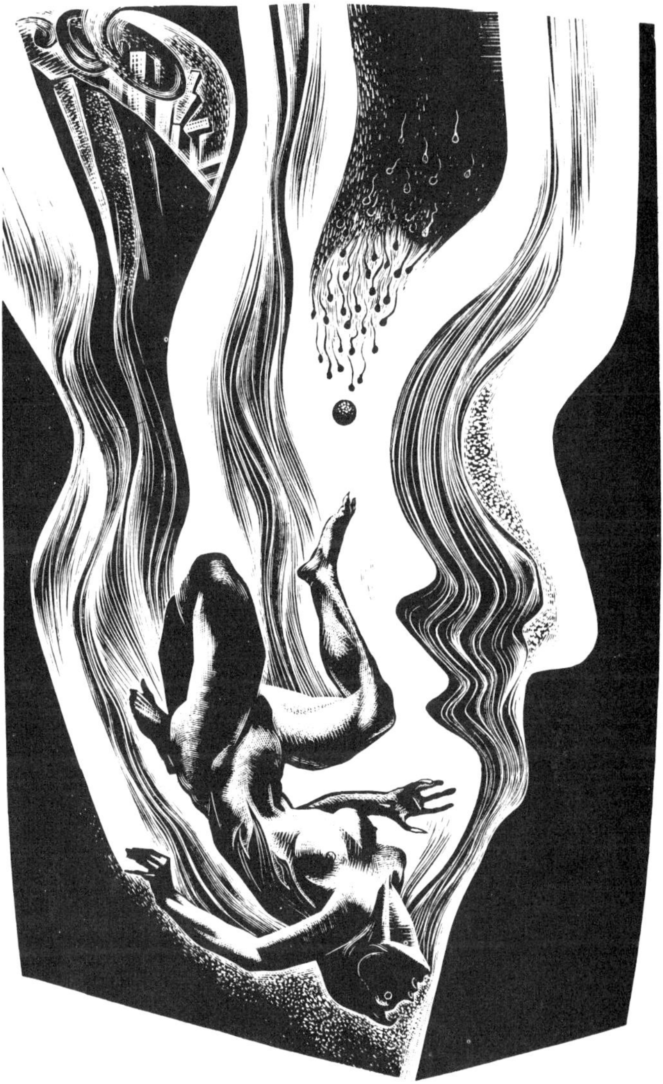

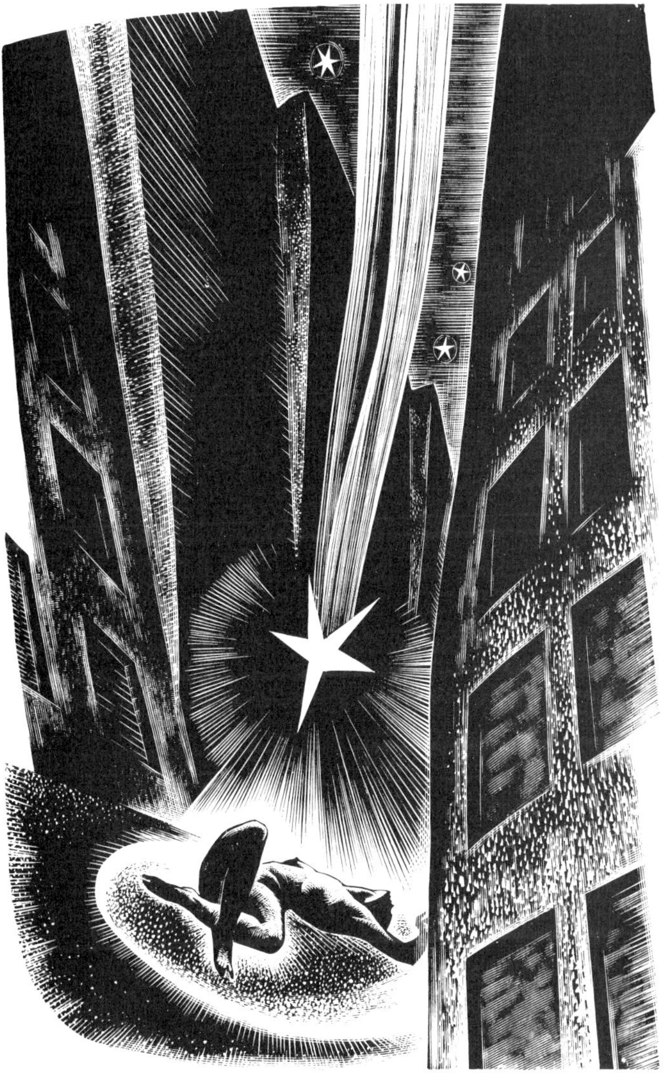

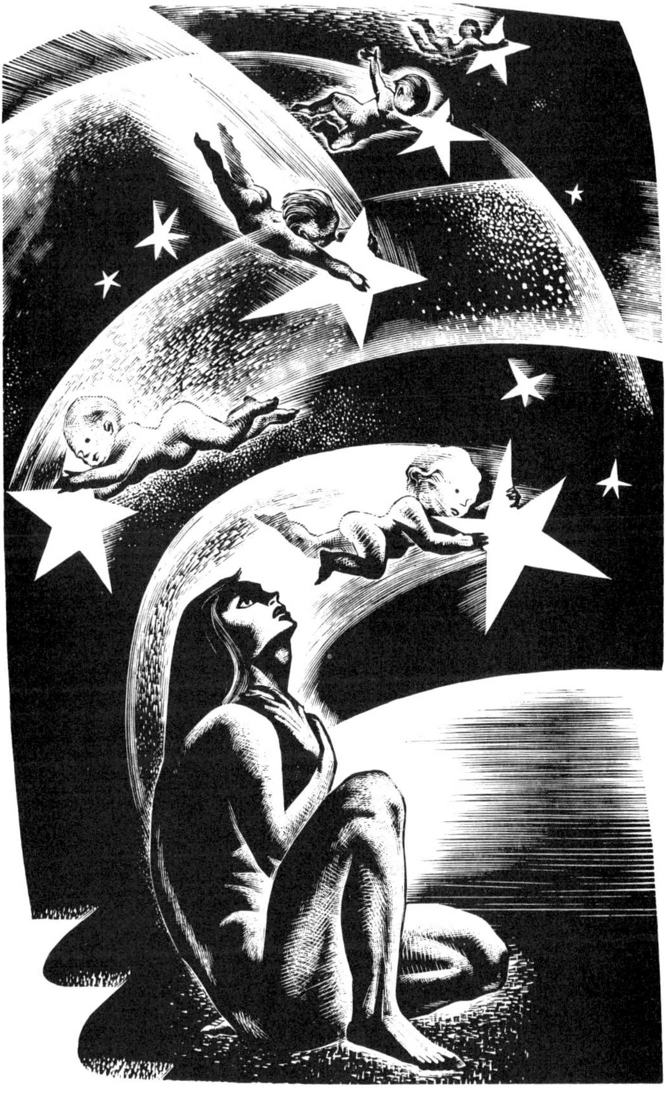

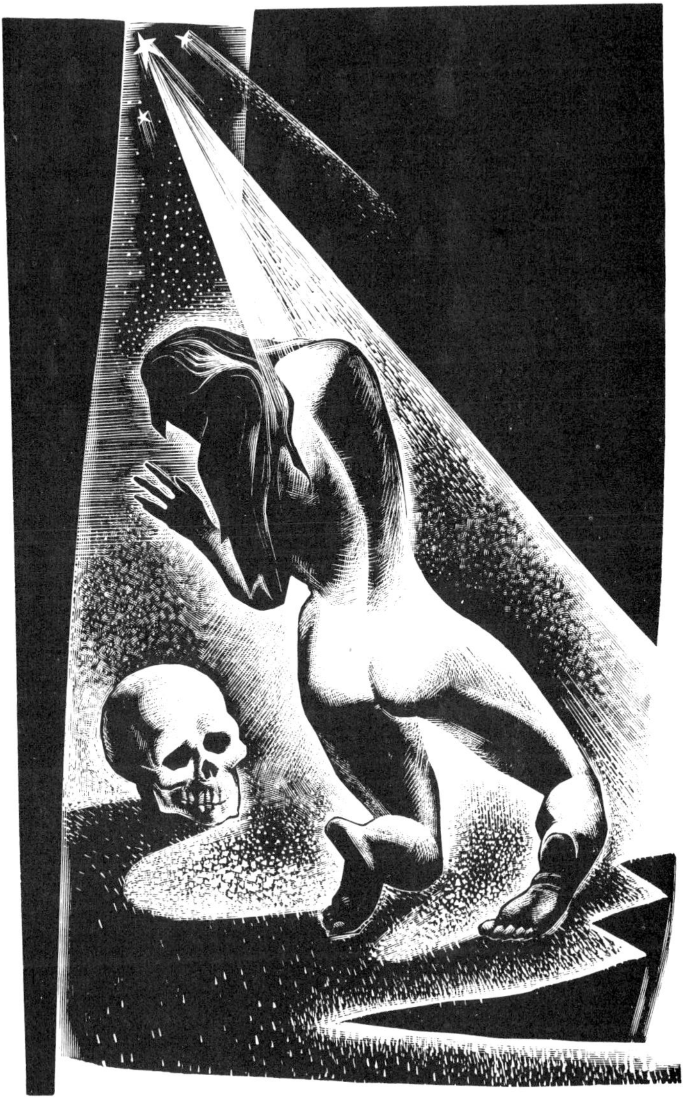

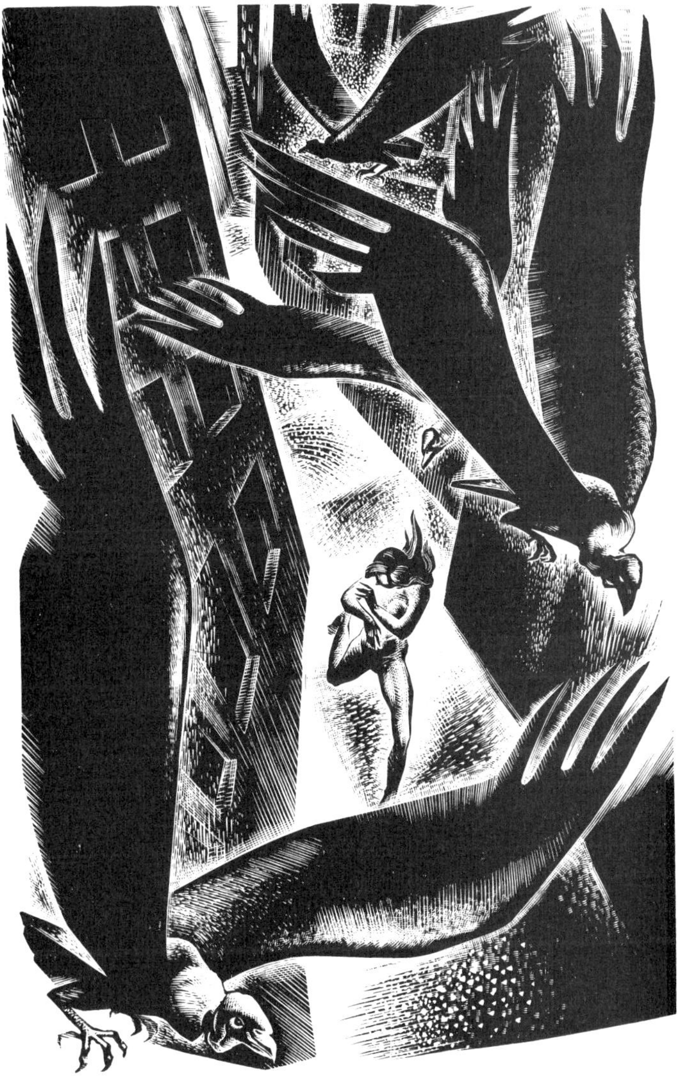

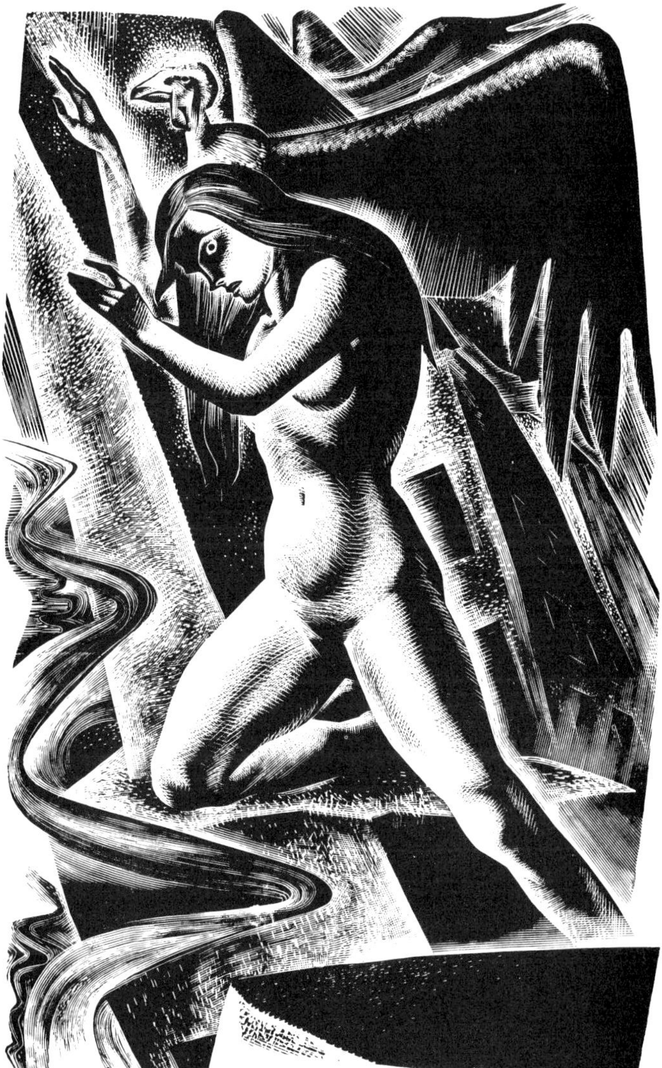

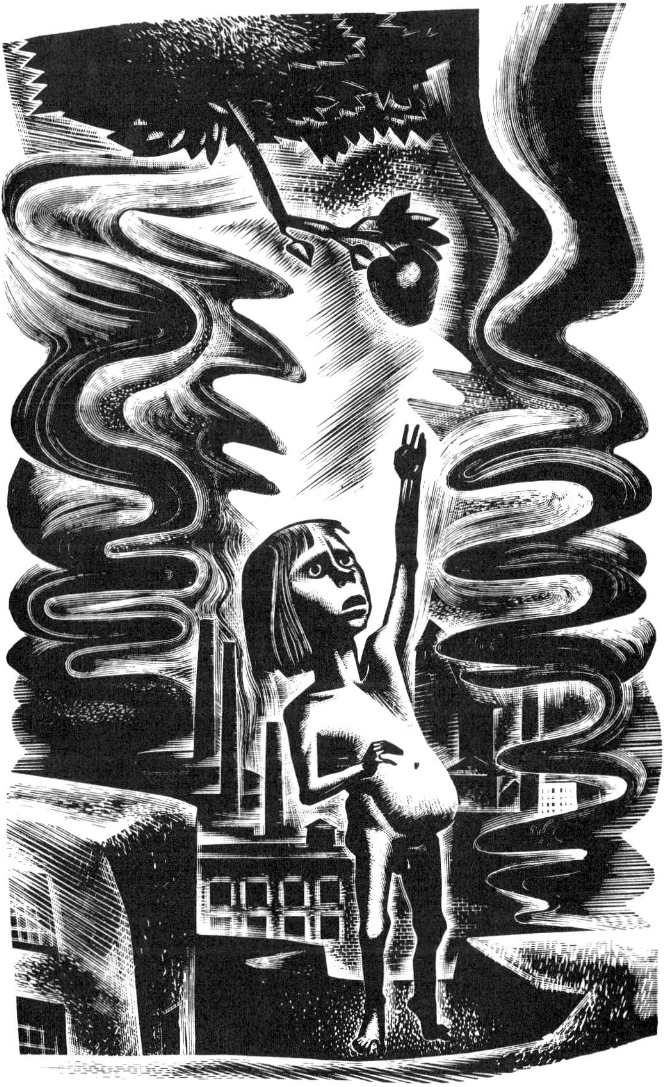

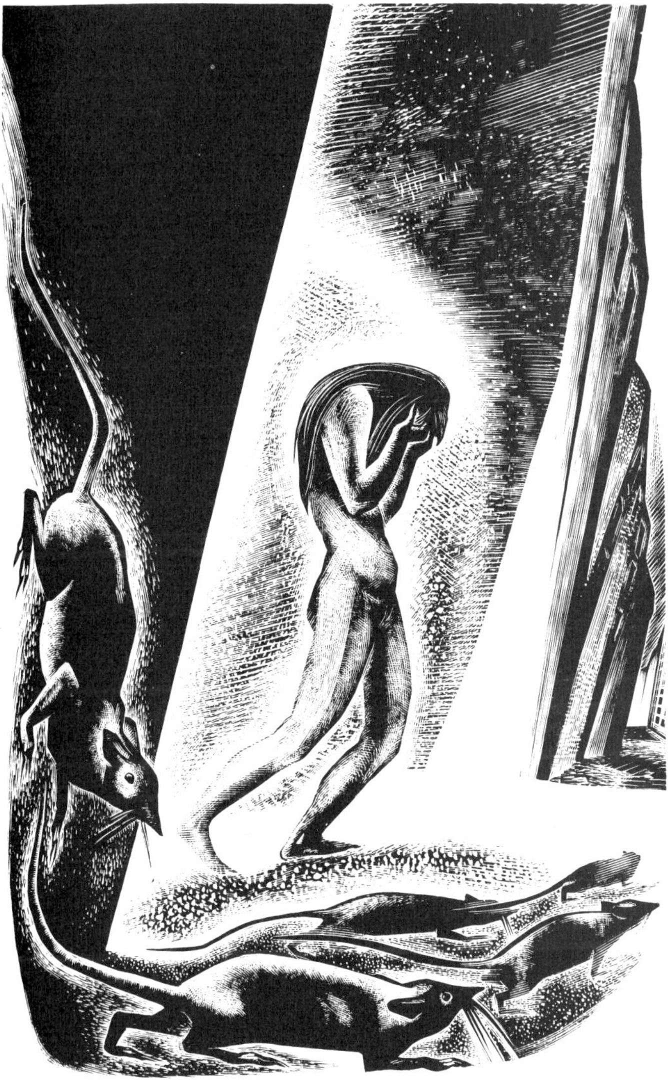

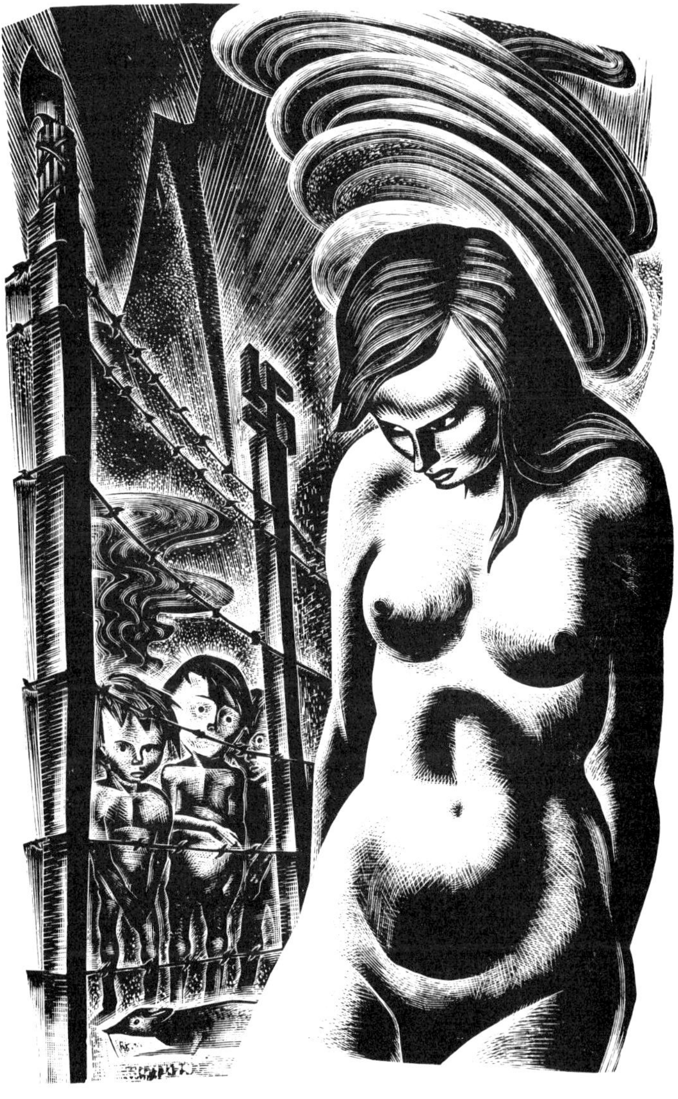

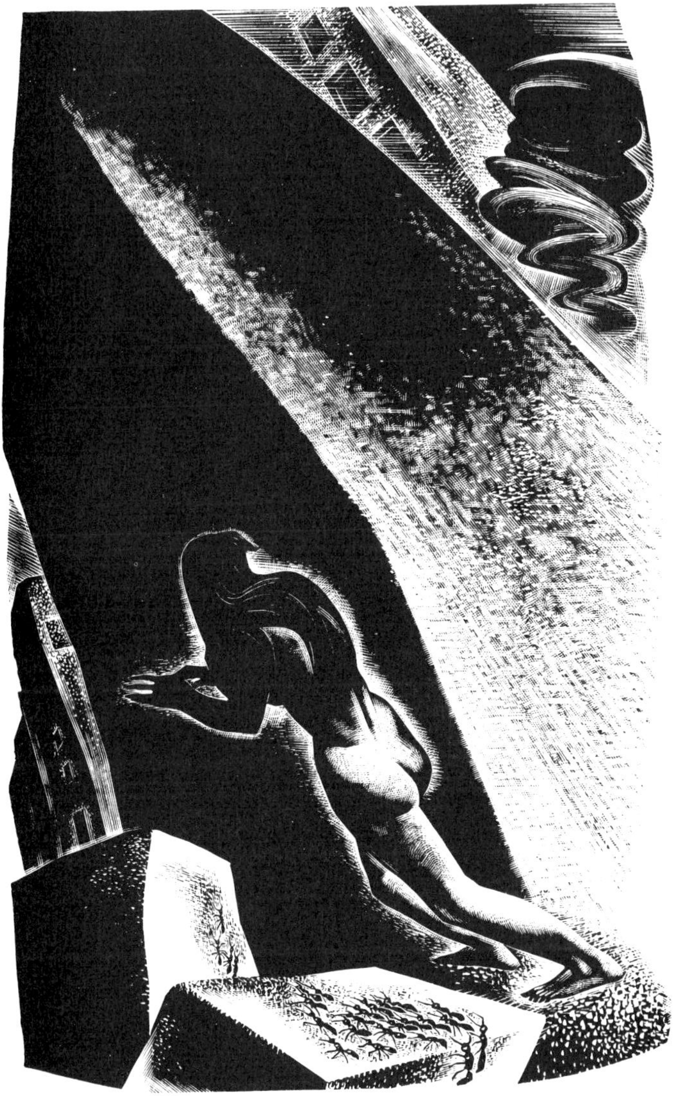

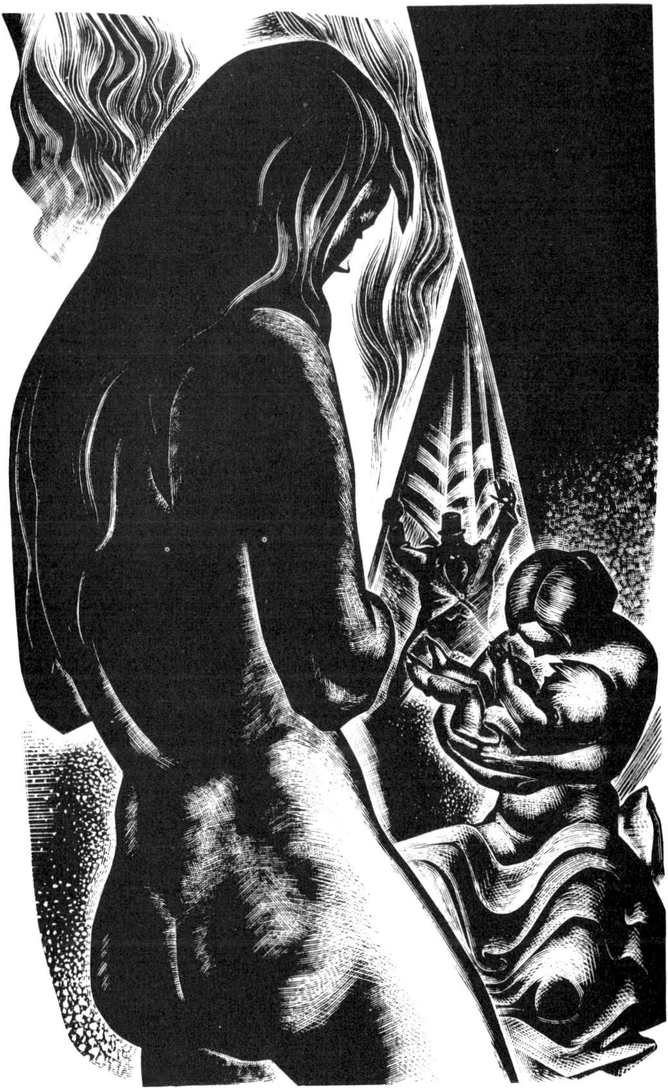

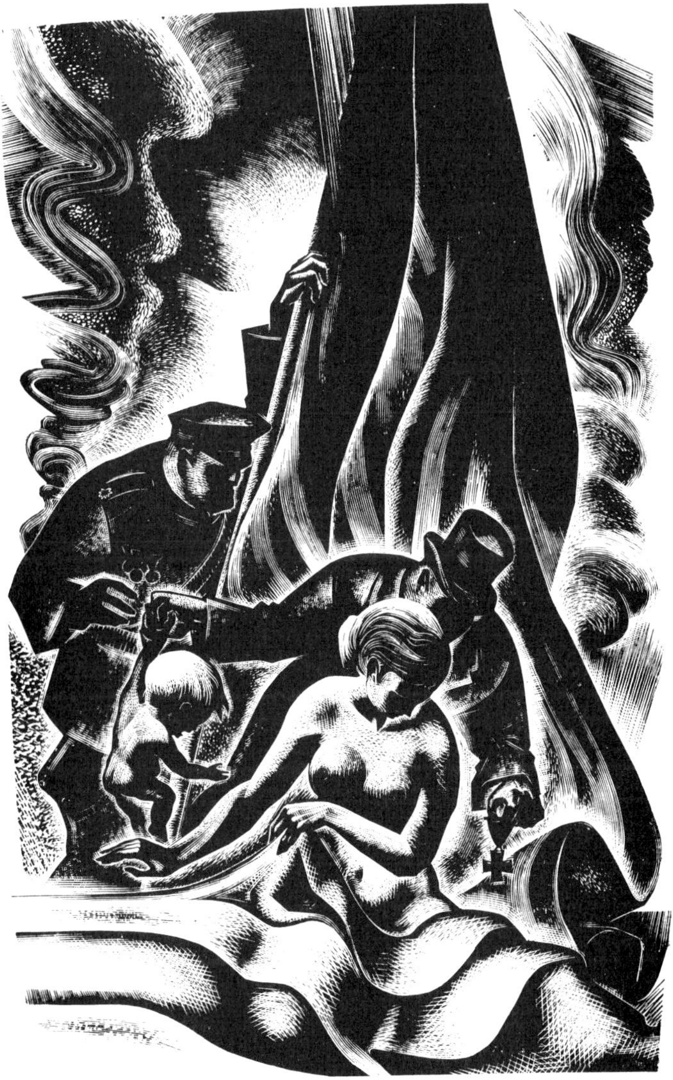

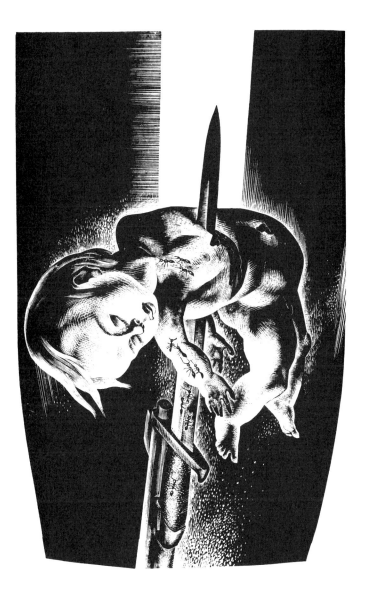

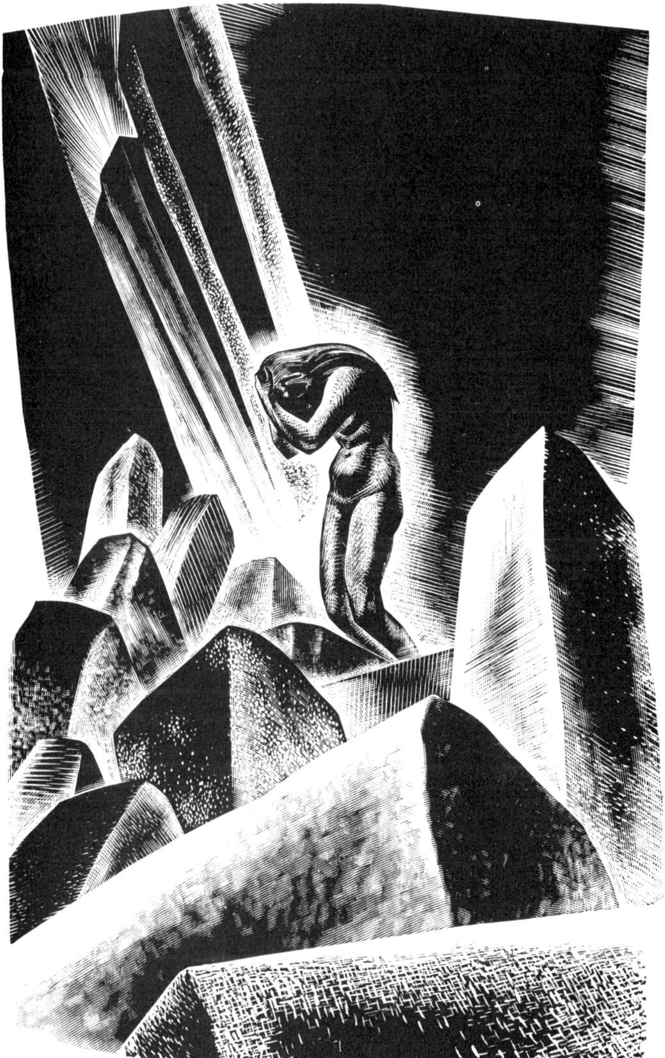

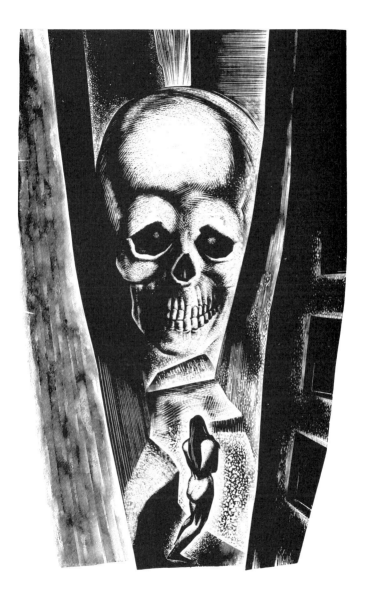

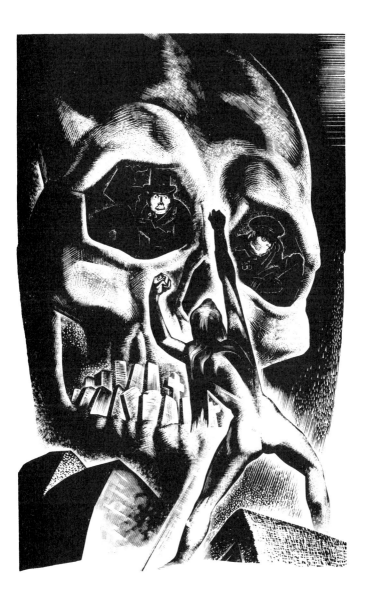

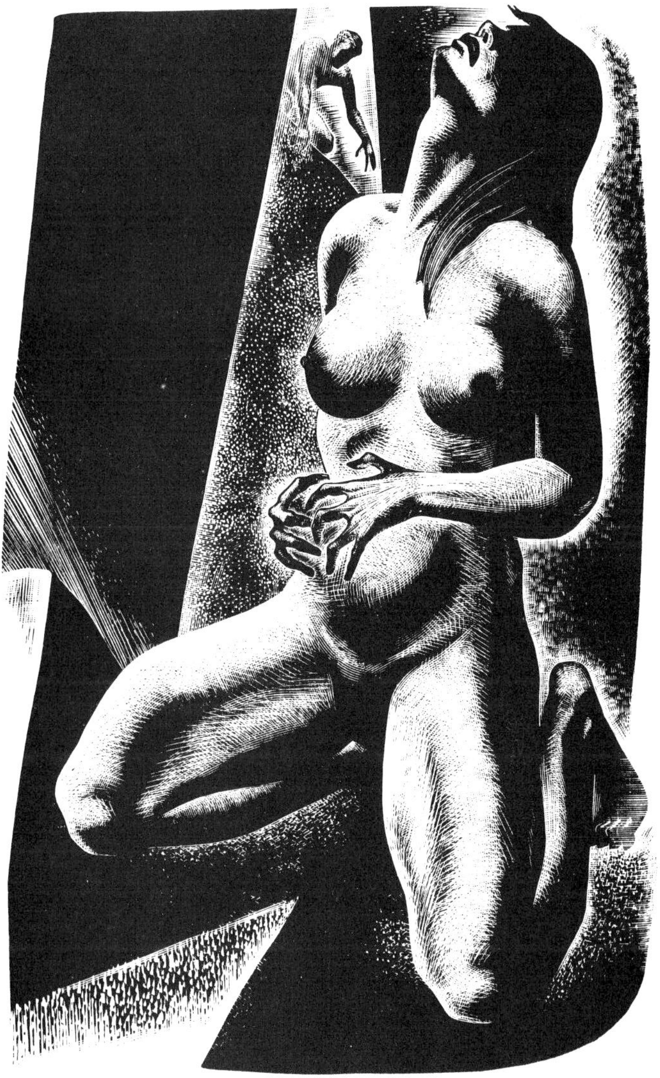

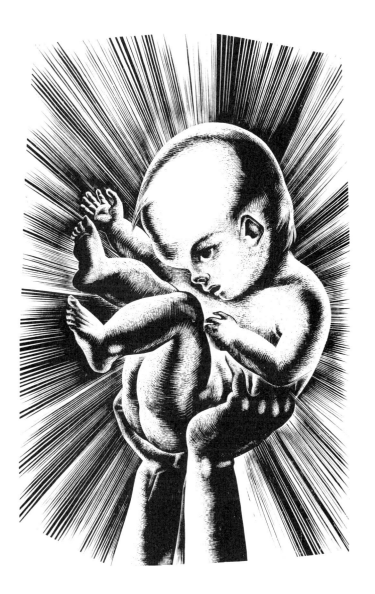

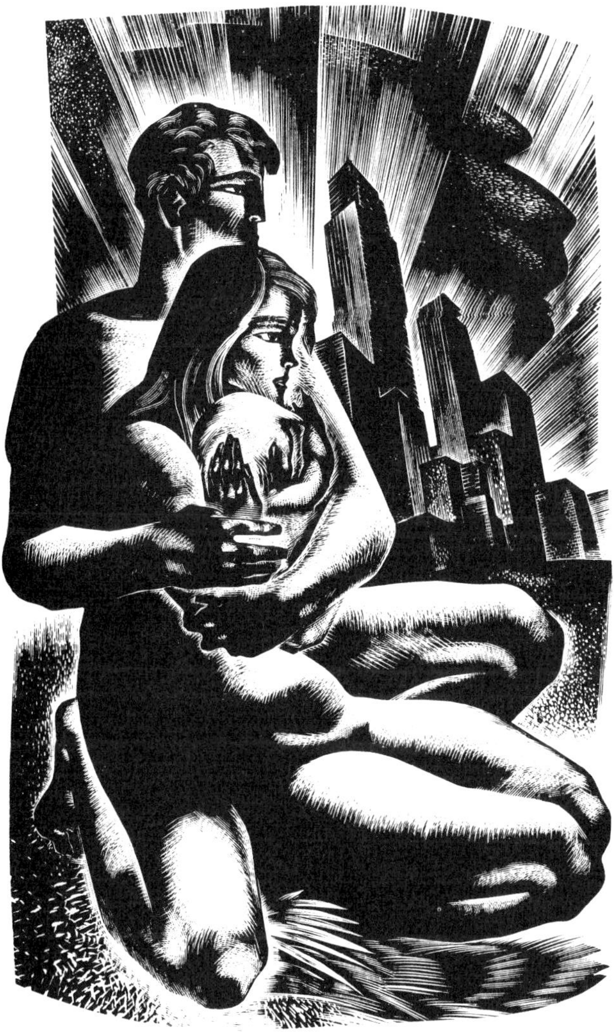

VERTIGO

A NOVEL IN WOODCUTS BY LYND WARD

RANDOM HOUSE · NEW YORK · 1937

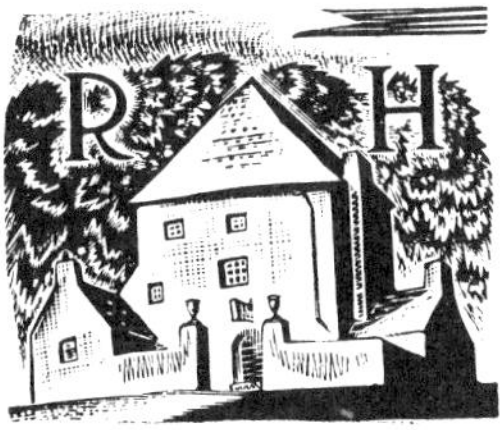
R H

THE GIRL

1929

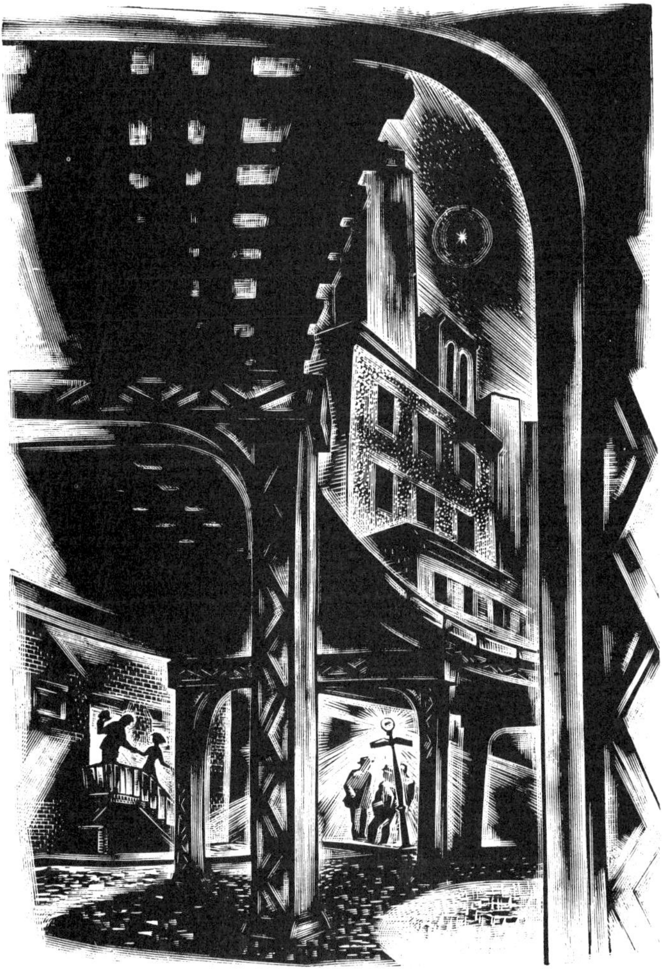

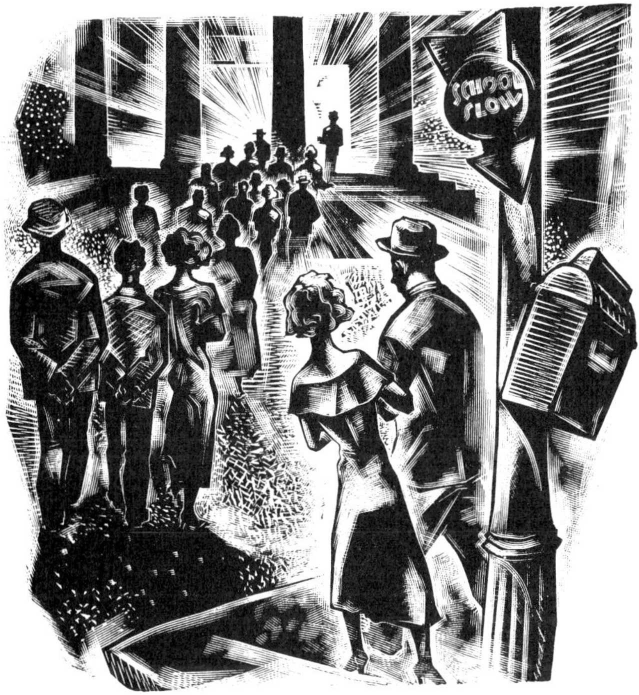
SCHOOL
SLOW

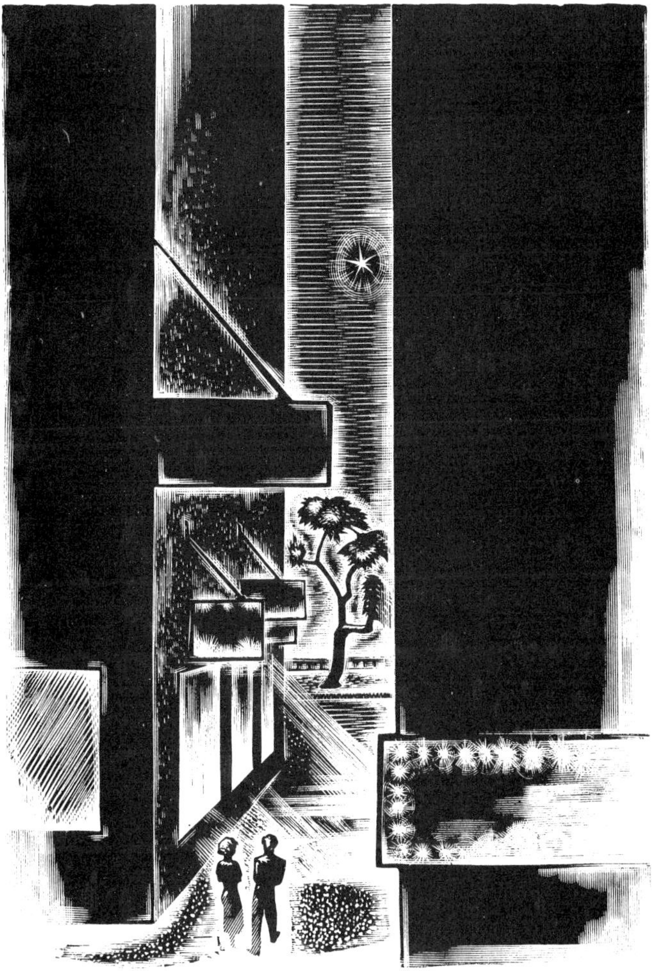

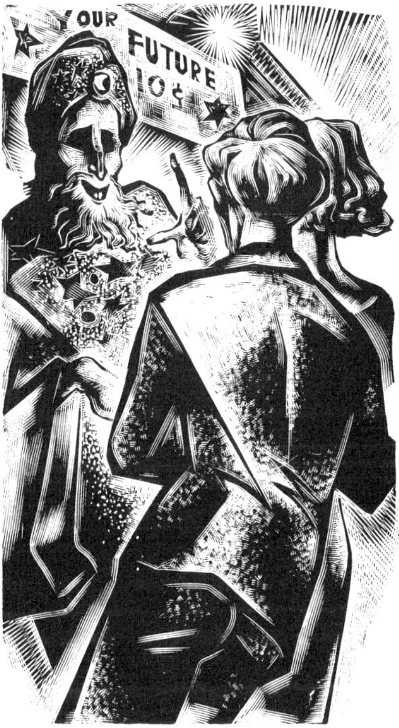
YOUR
FUTURE
10¢

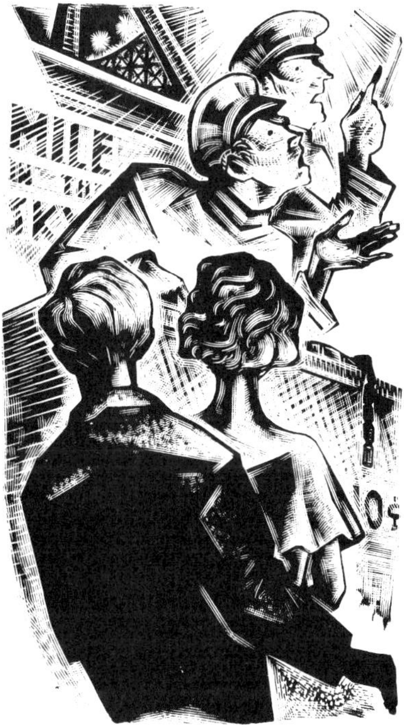
MILE

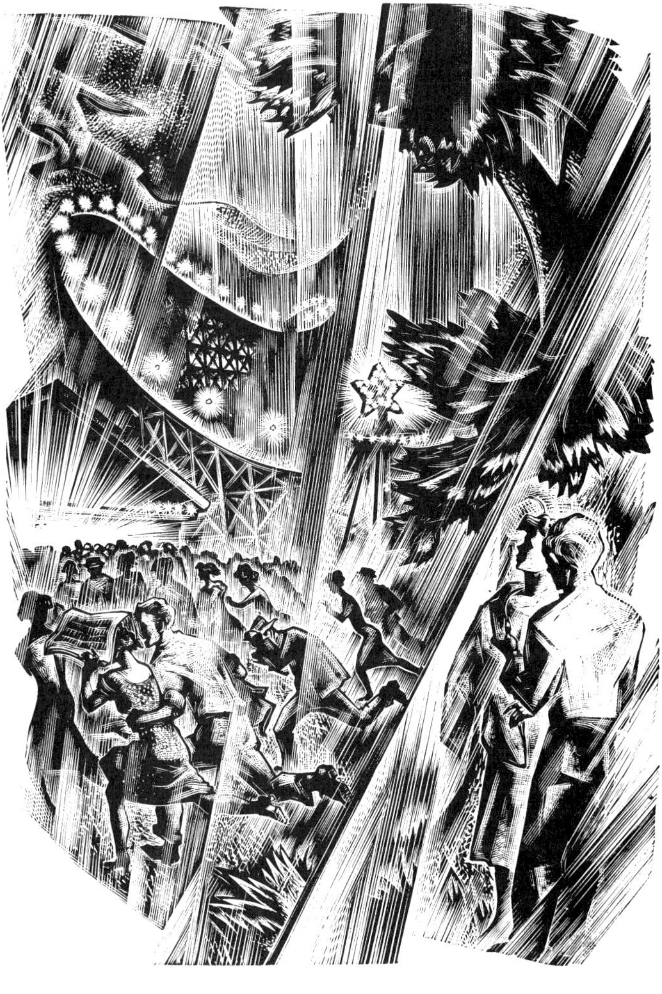

1930

1931

1932

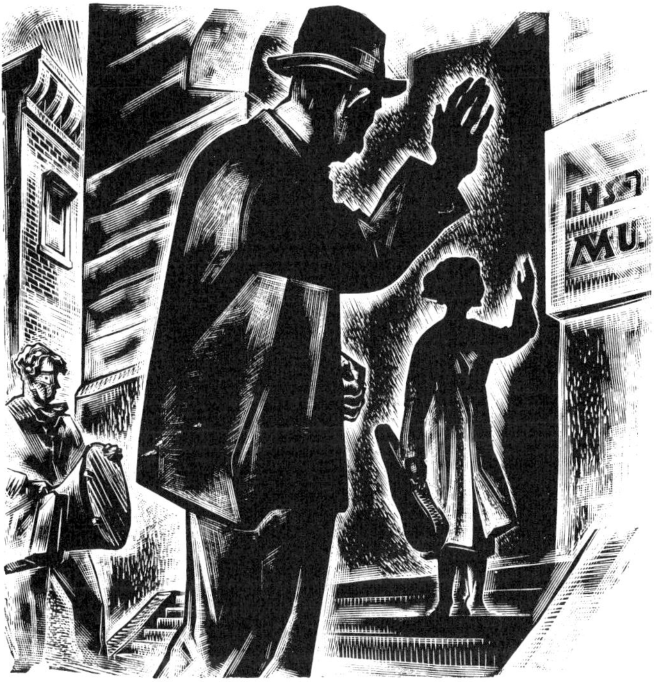
INS
MU

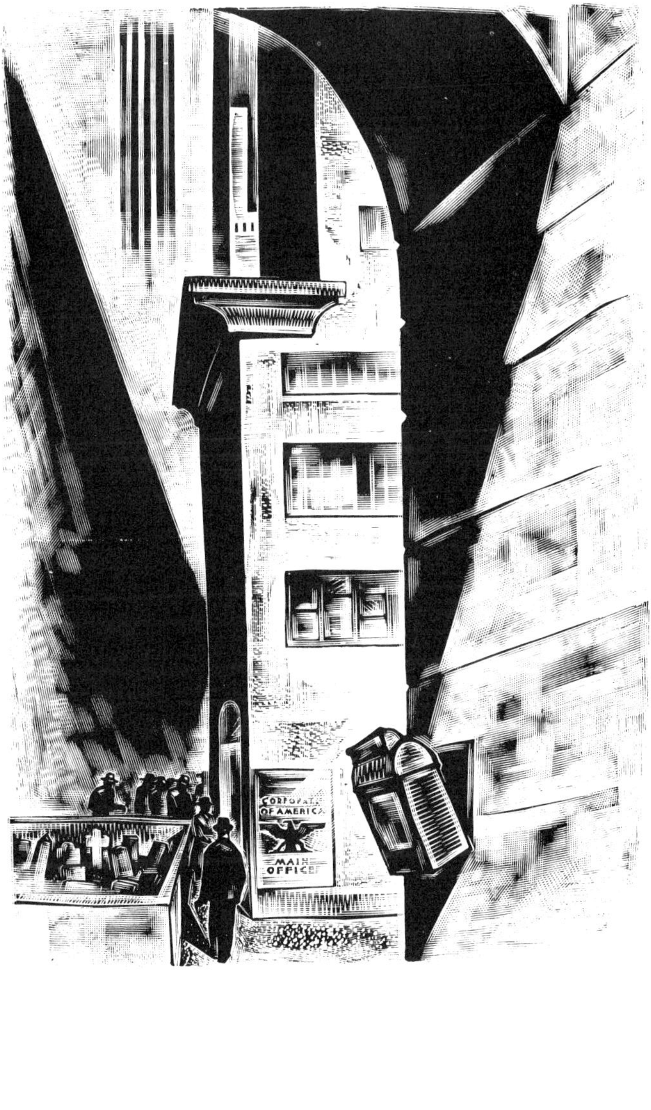
OF AMERICA
MAIN
OFFICE

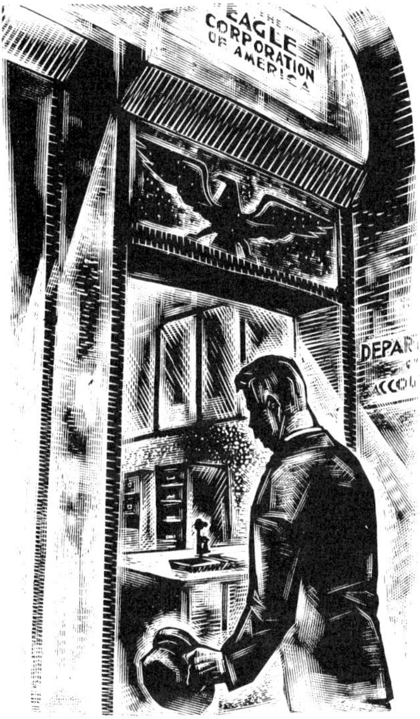
EAGLE
CORPORATION
OF AMERICA

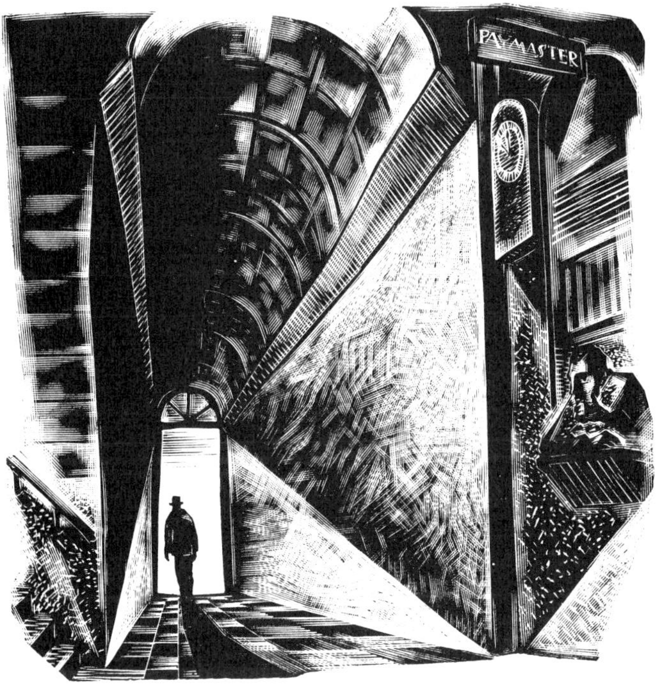
PAYMASTER

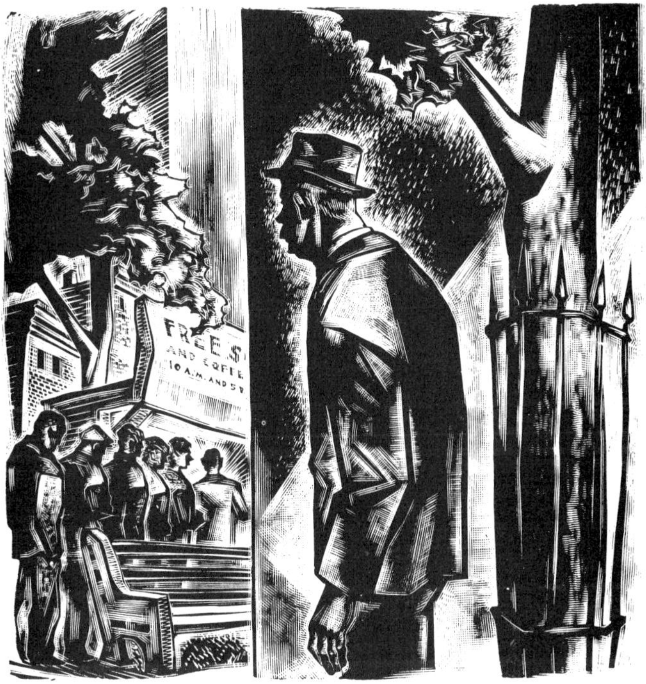
FREE S
AND COFFE
10 A.M. AND 5 P

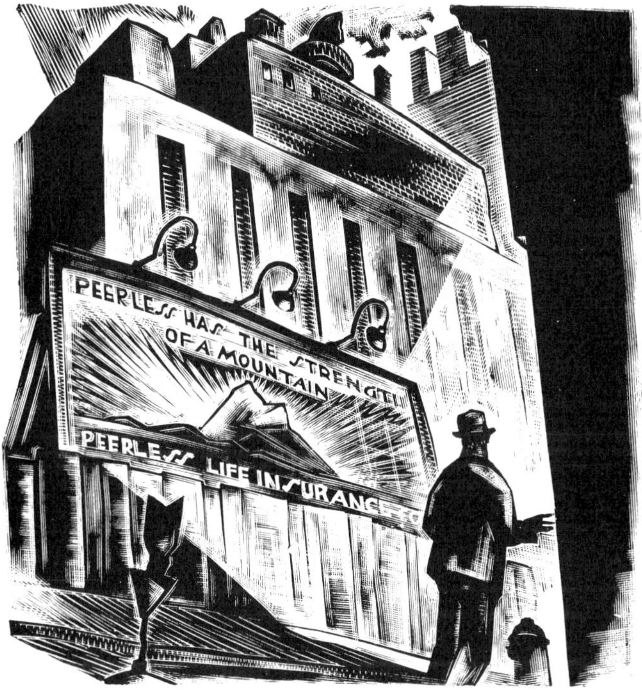
PEERLESS HAS THE STRENGTH
OF A MOUNTAIN
PEERLESS LIFE INSURANCE CO

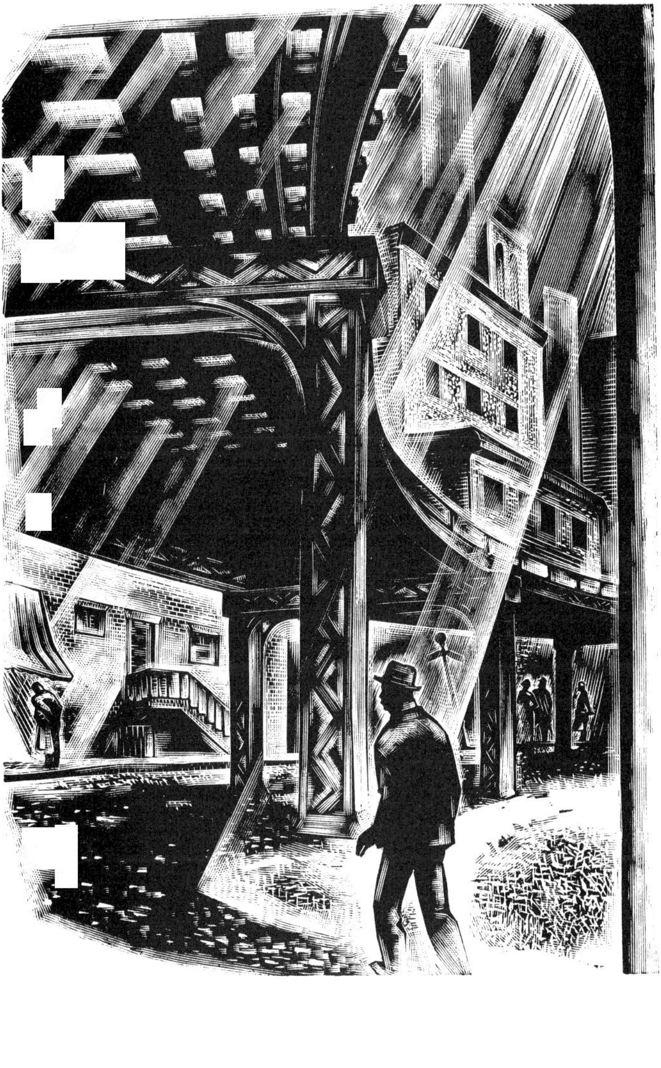

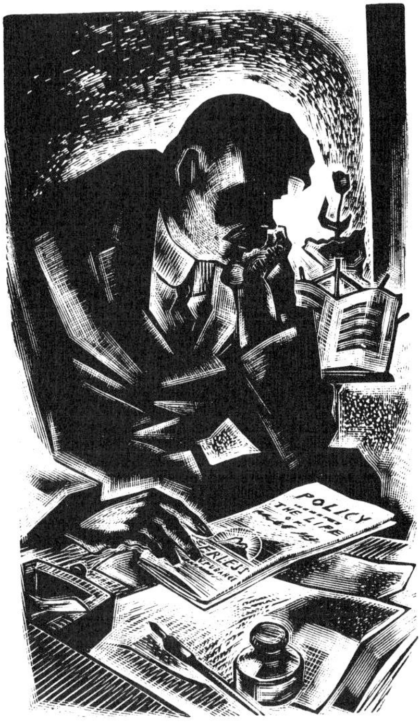
POLICY
THE LIFE

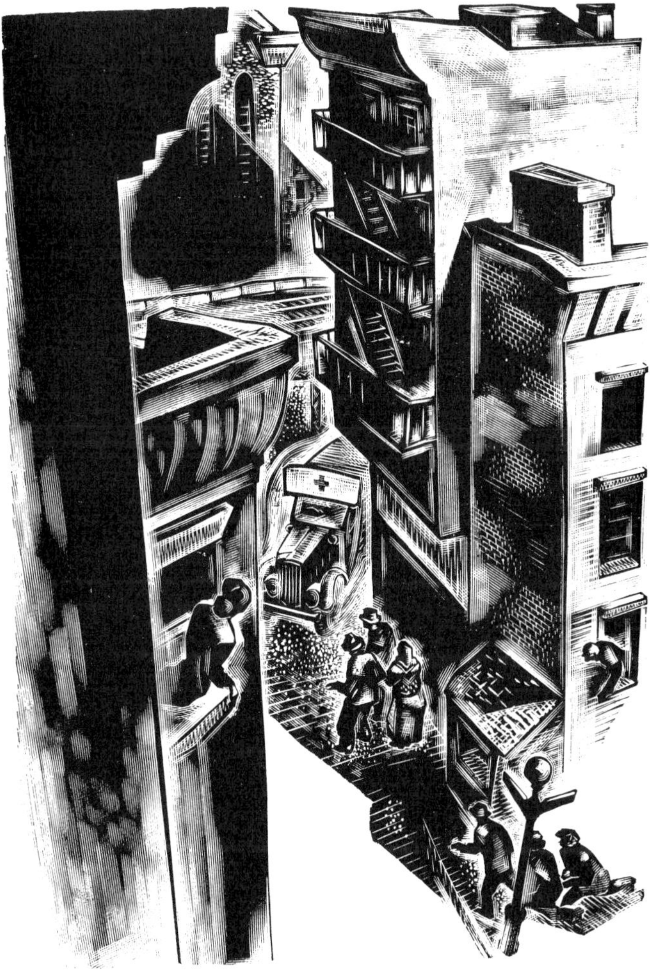

1933

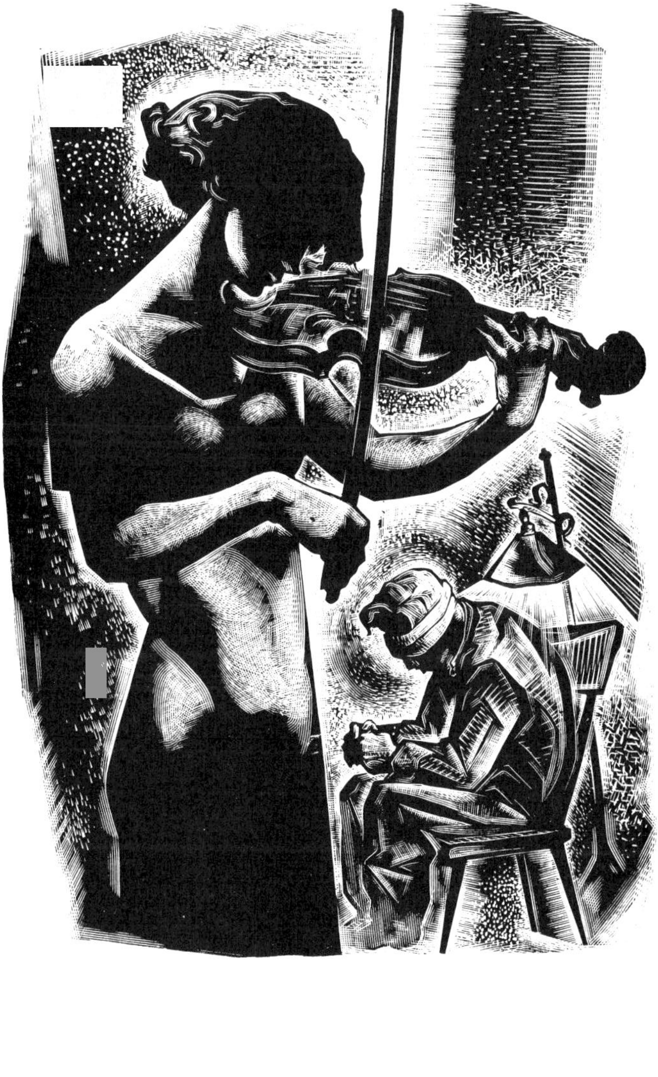

1934

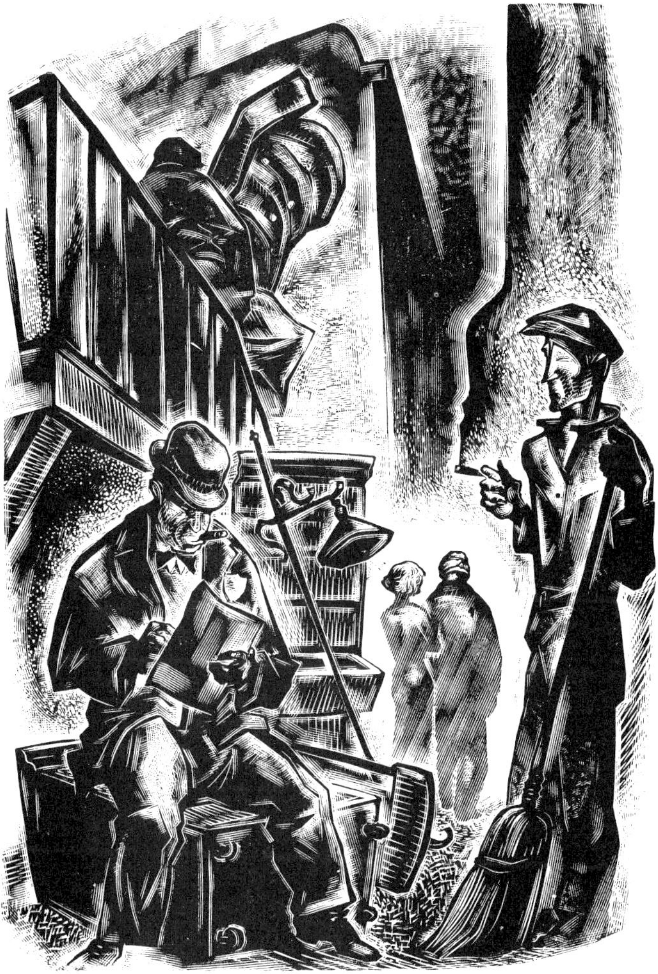

1935

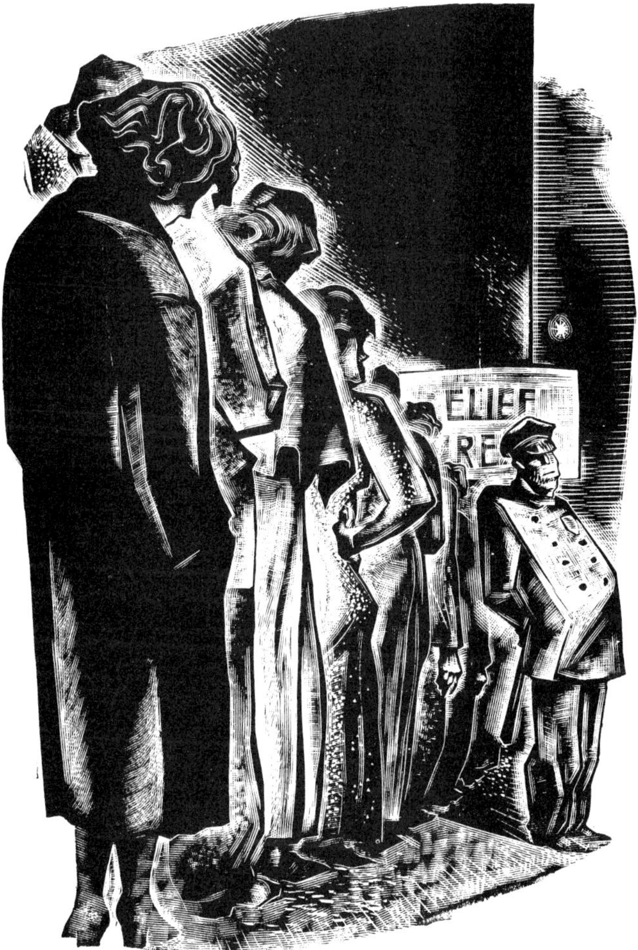
ELIEF
RE

AN ELDERLY GENTLEMAN

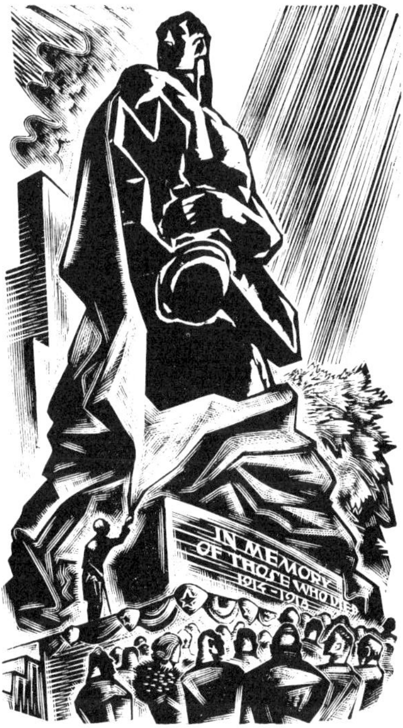
IN MEMORY
OF THOSE WHO DIED
1914 - 1918

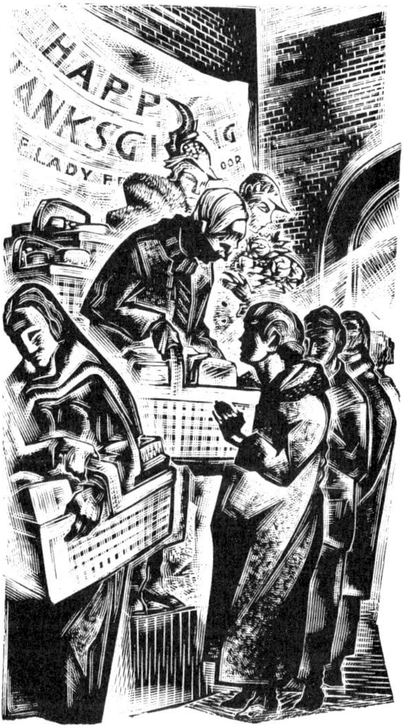
HAPP
NKSGI
G
LADY F
OOR

JANUARY

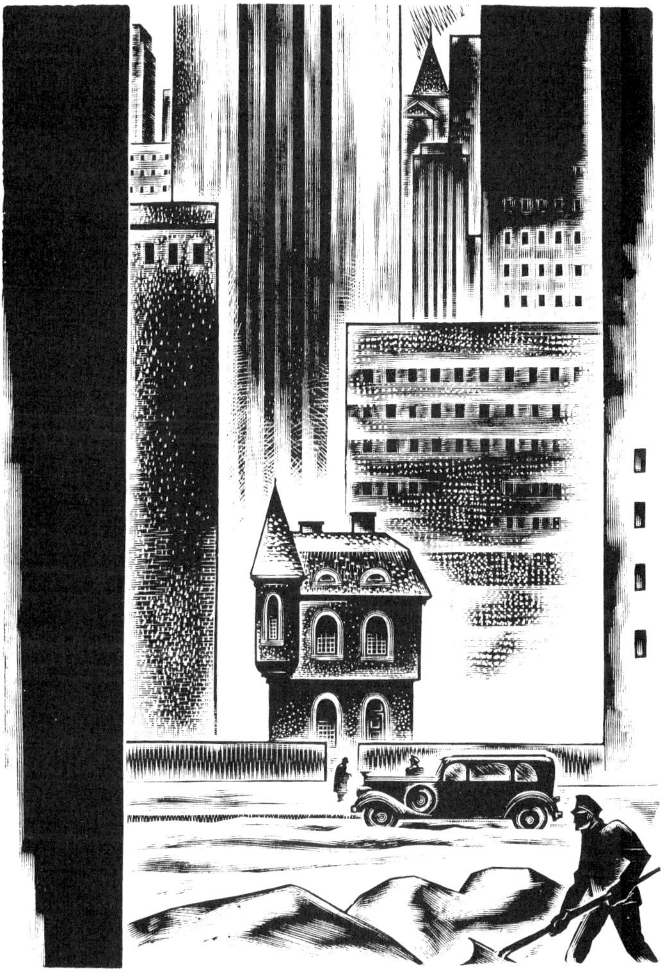

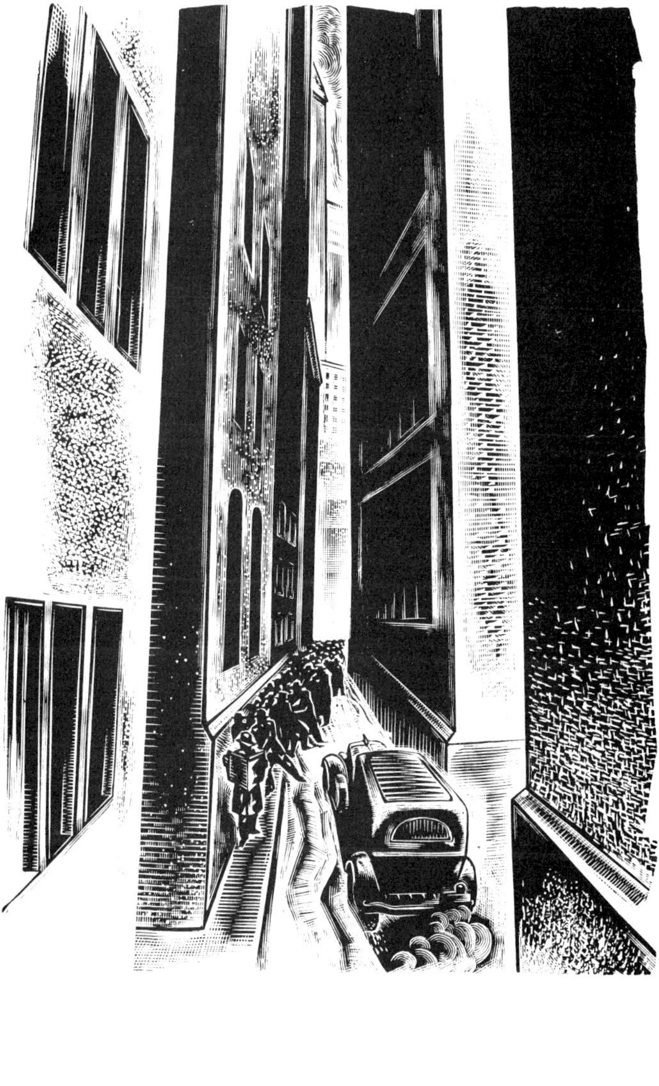

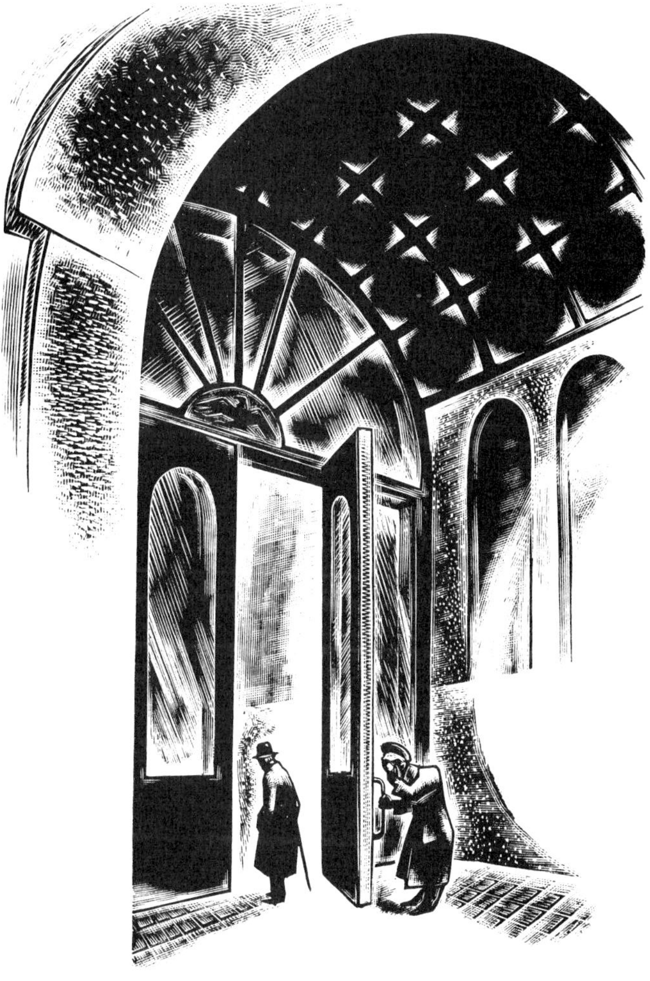

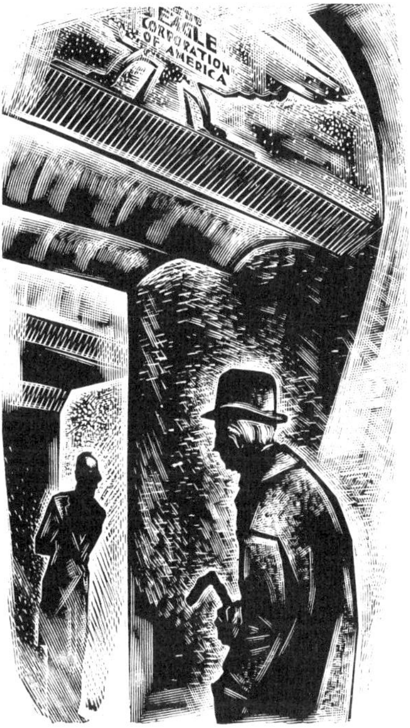
EAGLE
CORPORATION
OF AMERICA

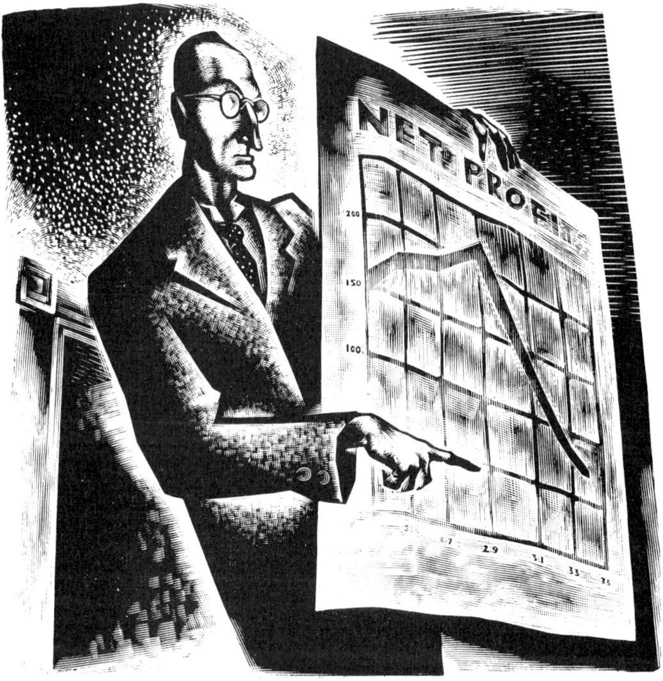
NET PROF
200
150
100
29
31
33

·

FEBRUARY

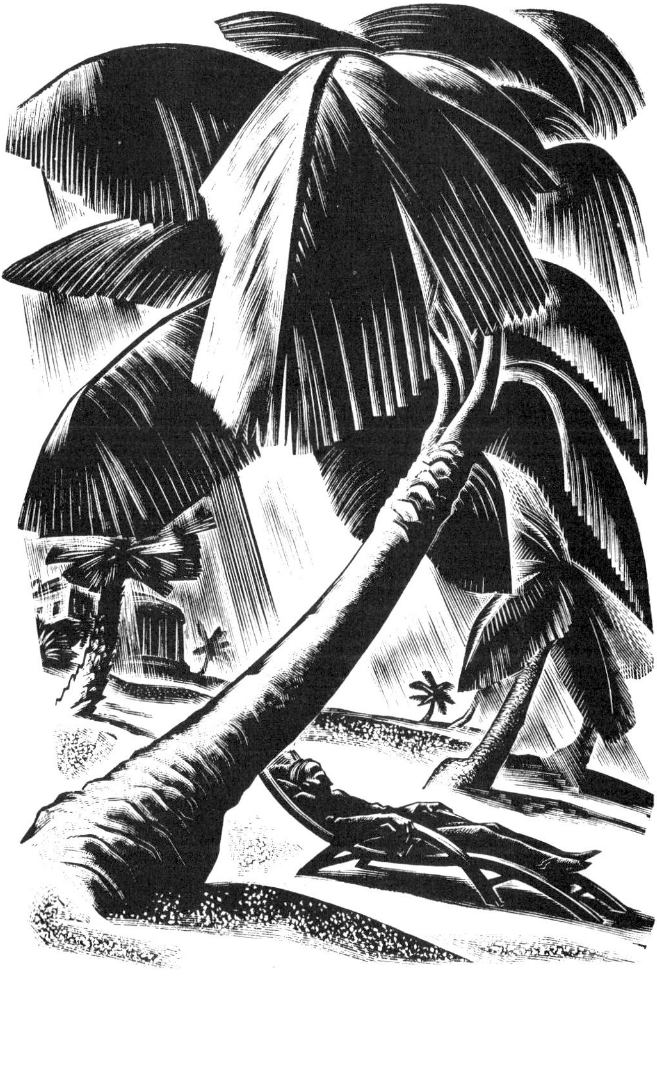

MARCH

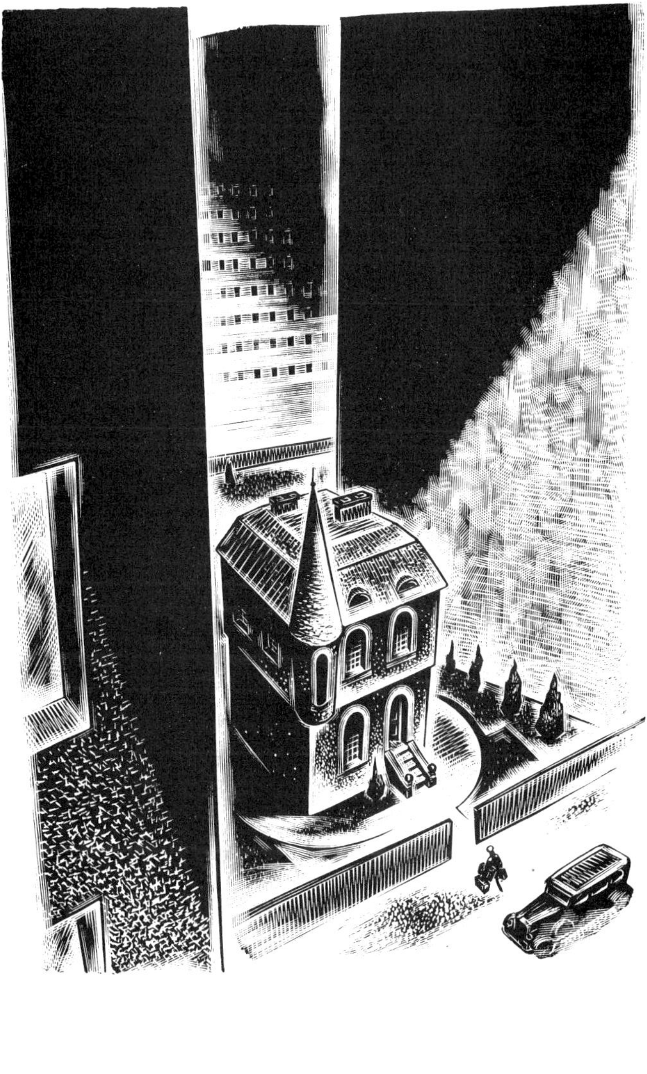

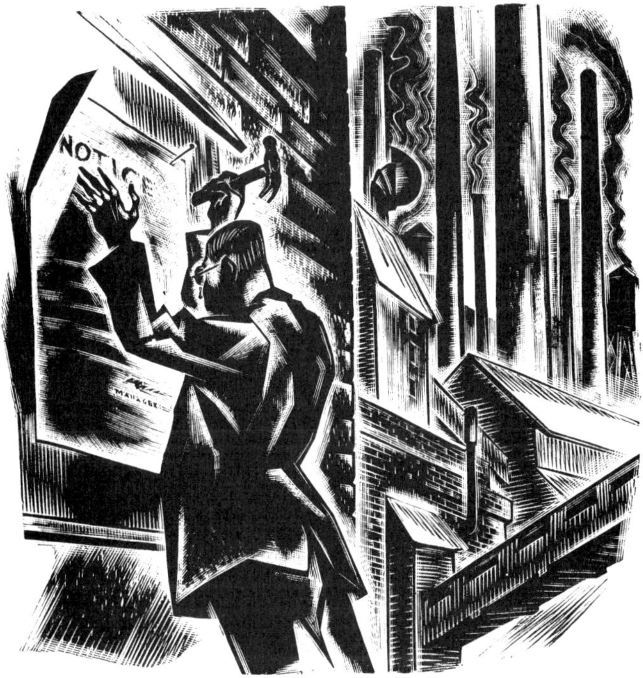
NOTICE
MANAGER

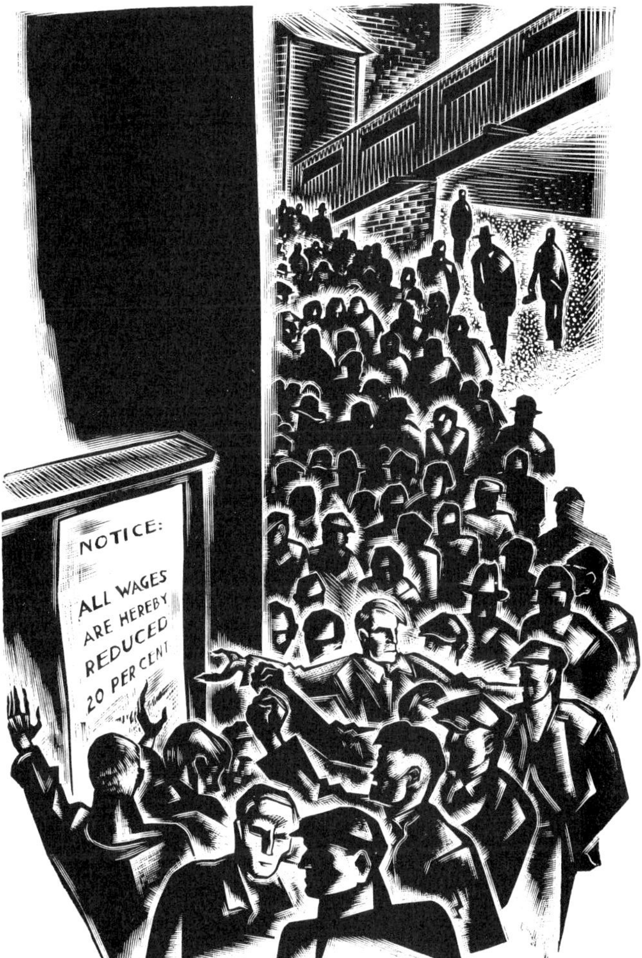
NOTICE:
ALL WAGES
ARE HEREBY
REDUCED
20 PER CENT

APRIL

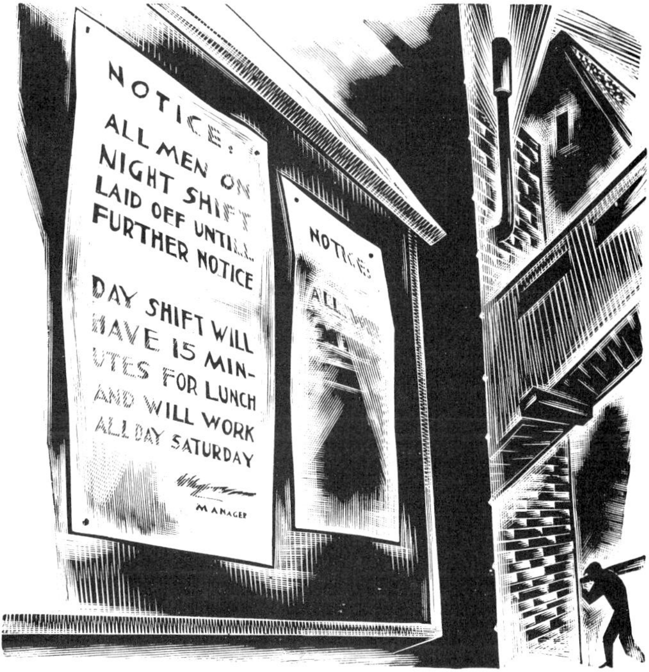
NOTICE:
ALL MEN ON
NIGHT SHIFT
LAID OFF UNTILL
FURTHER NOTICE
DAY SHIFT WILL
HAVE 15 MIN-
UTES FOR LUNCH
AND WILL WORK
ALL DAY SATURDAY
MANAGER

MAY

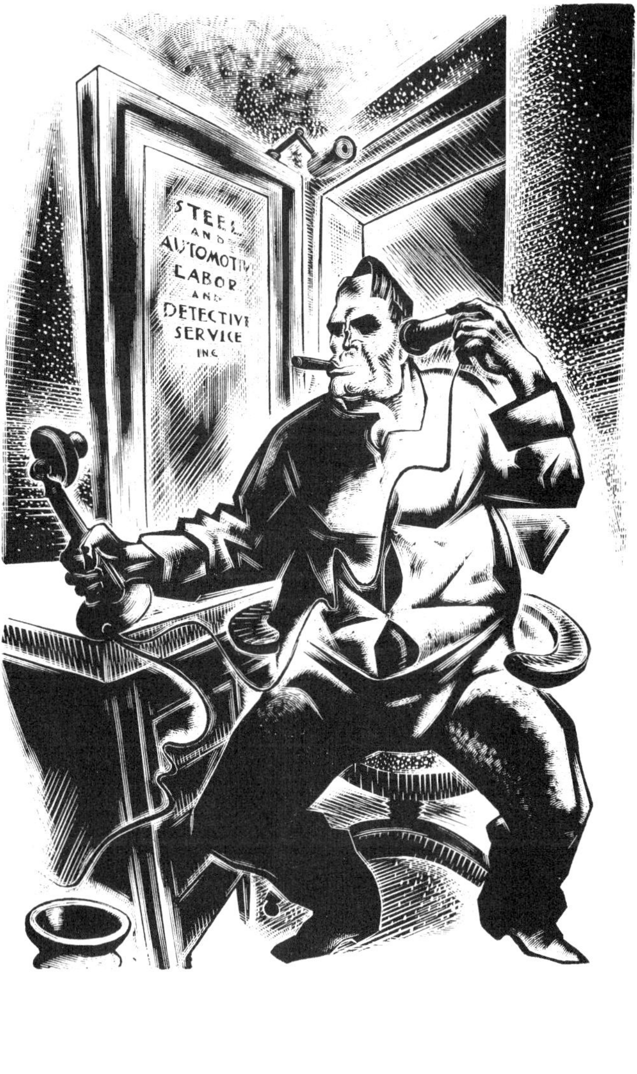
STEEL
AND
AUTOMOTIV
LABOR
AND
DETECTIVE
SERVICE
INC

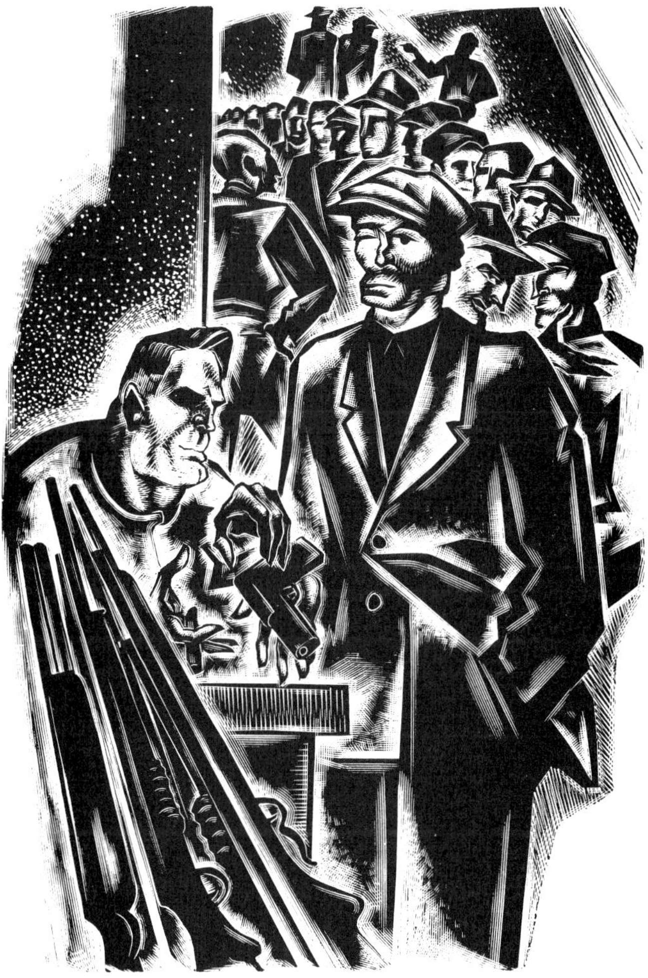

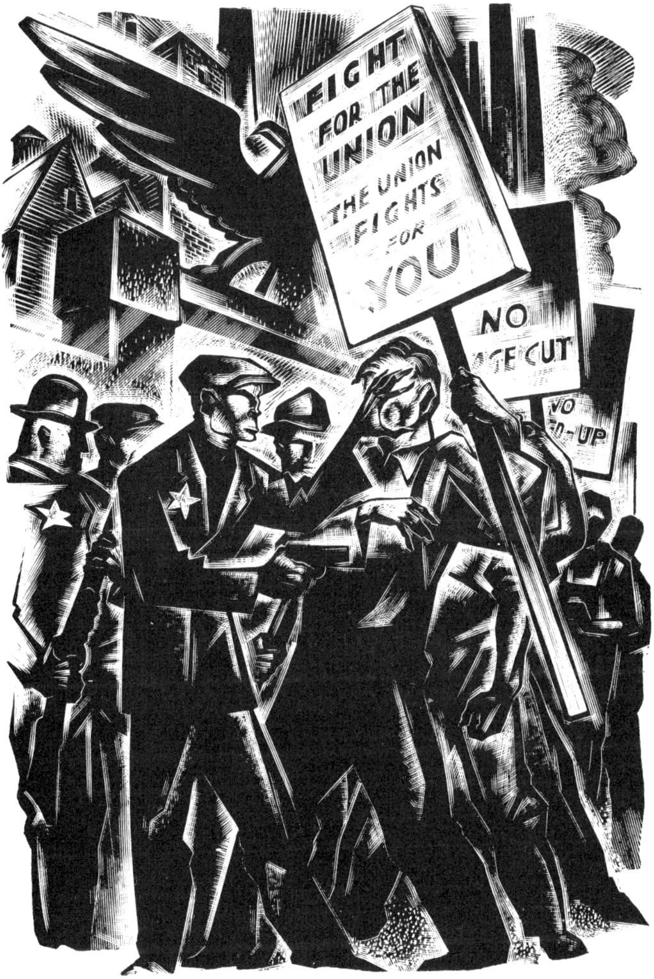
FIGHT FOR THE UNION
THE UNION FIGHTS FOR YOU
NO
NO

JUNE

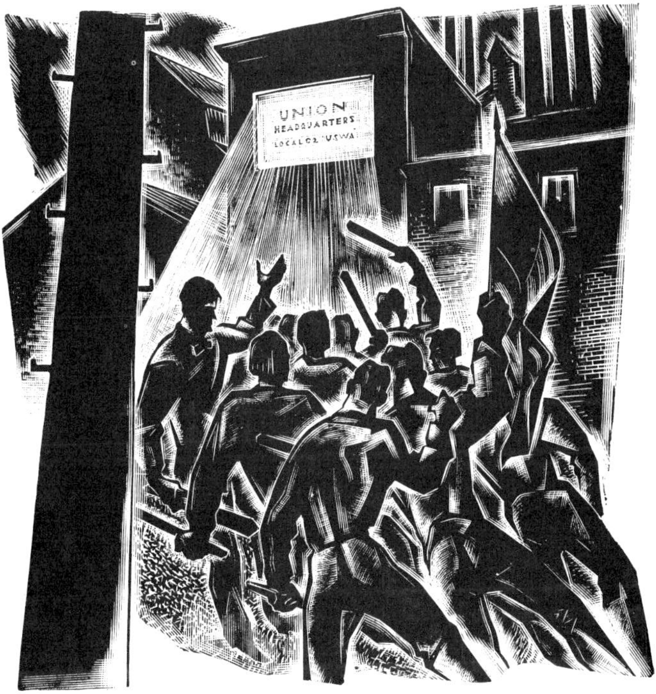
UNION
HEADQUARTERS
LOCAL 62 USWA

JULY

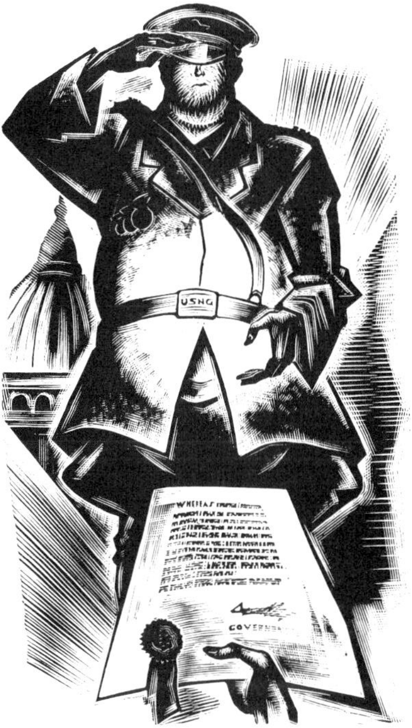
USNG
WHEREAS

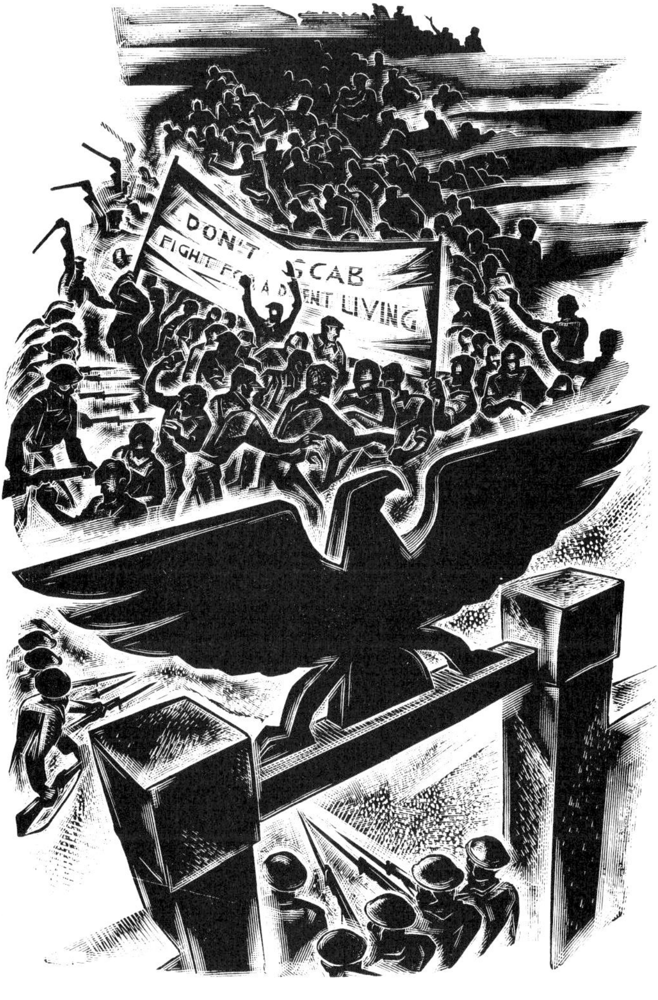
DON'T
SCAB
FIGHT
LIVING

AUGUST

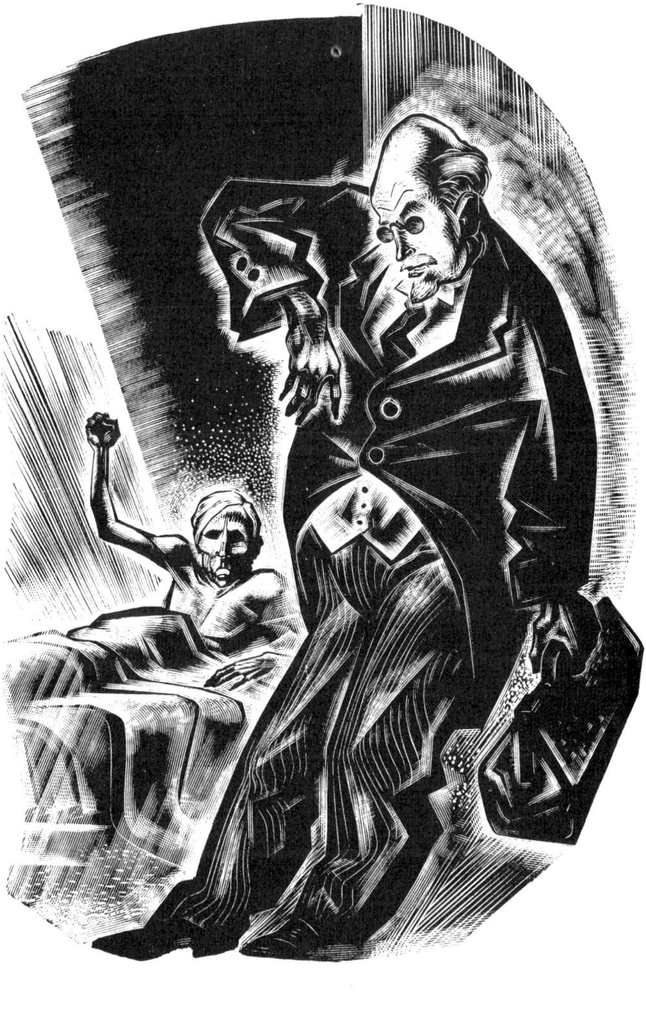

SEPTEMBER

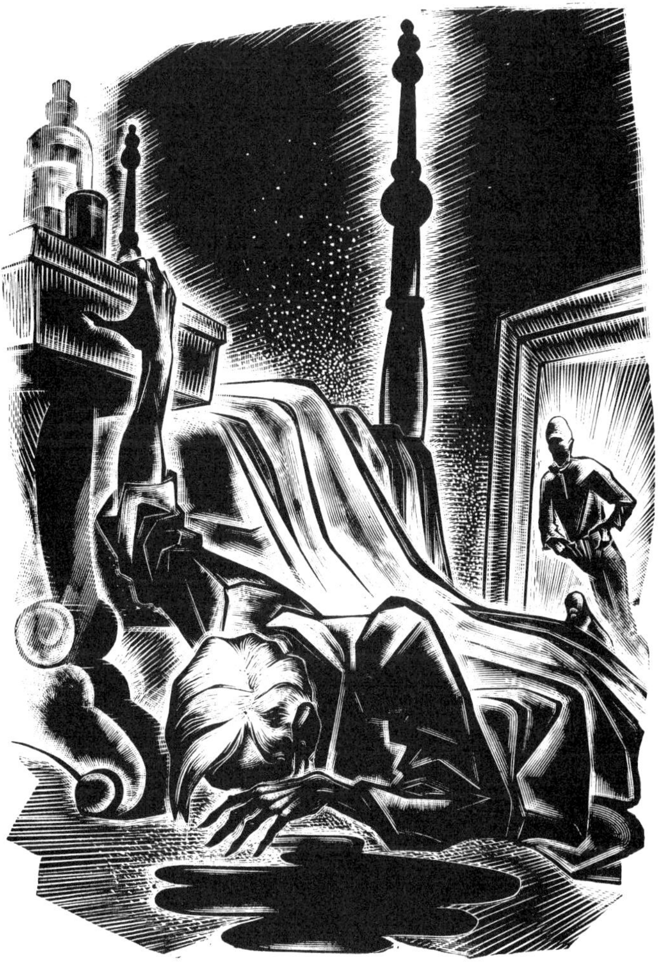

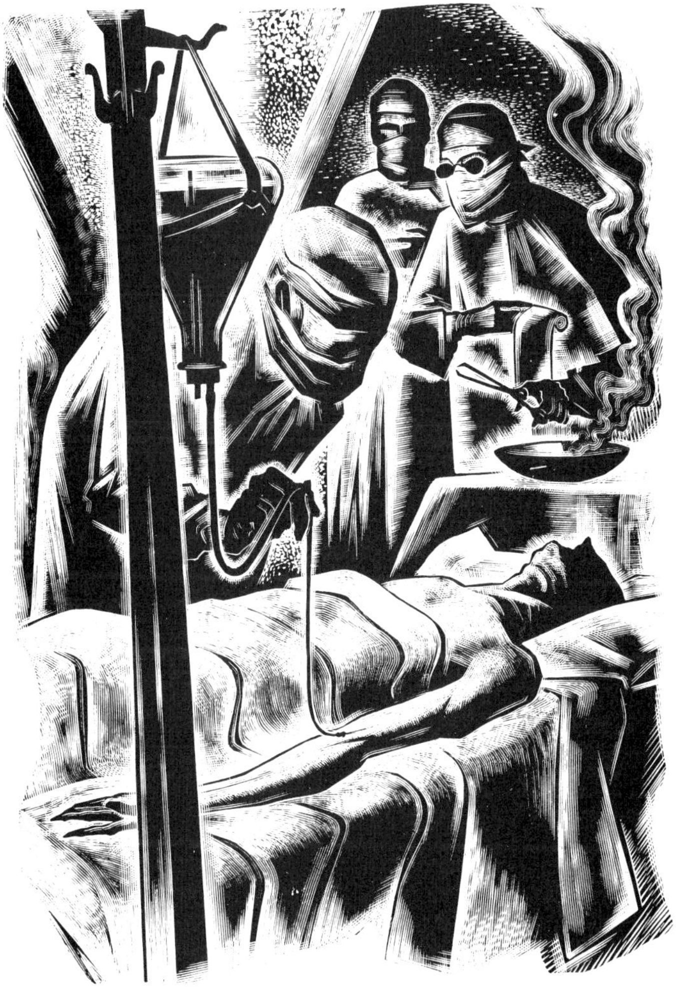

OCTOBER

NOVEMBER

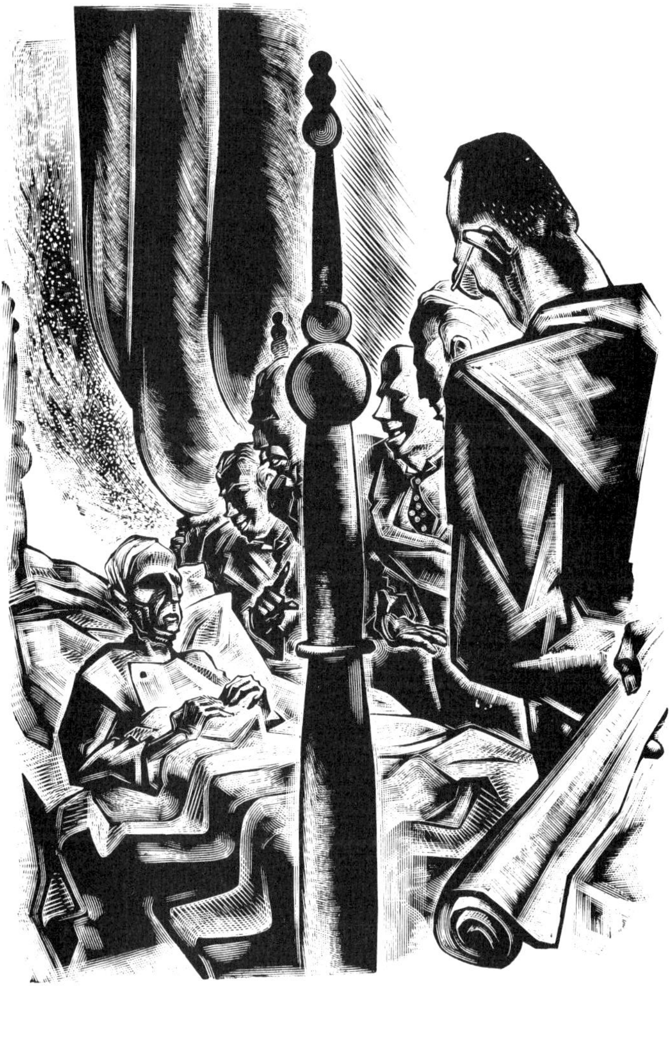

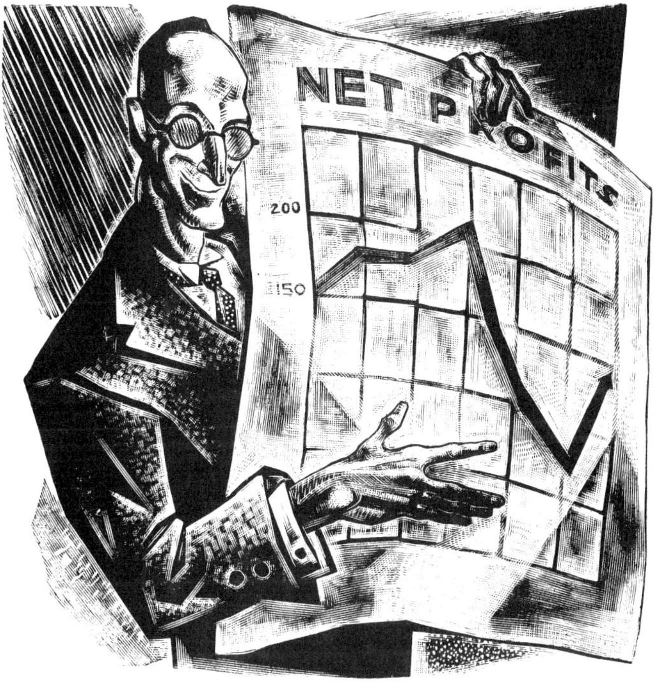
NET PROFITS
200
150

DECEMBER

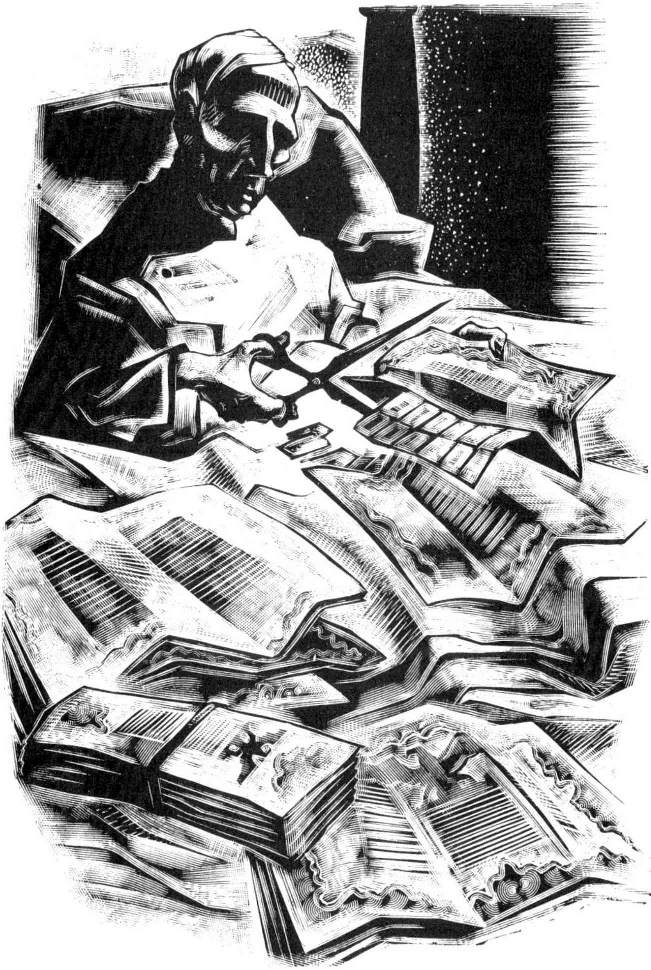

THE BOY

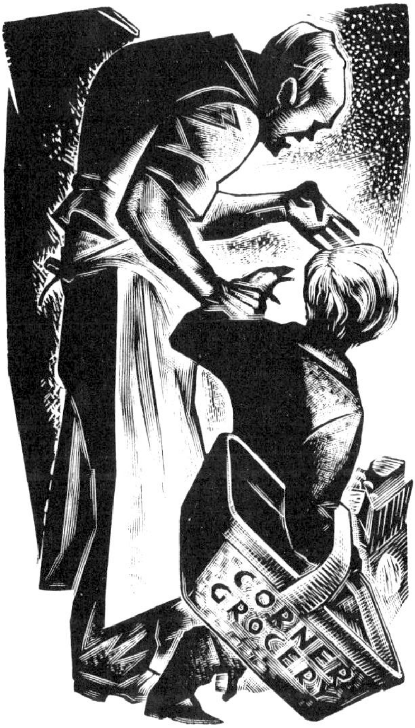
CORNER
GROCERY

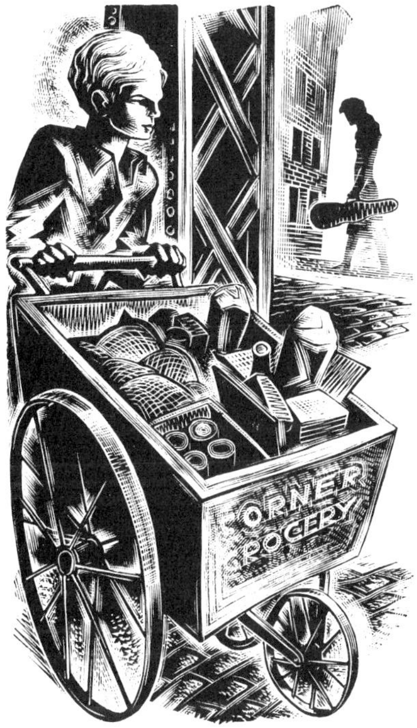
ORNER
ROCERY

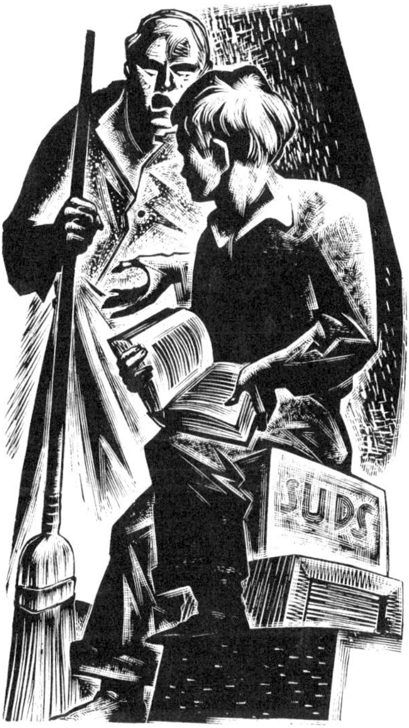
SUDS

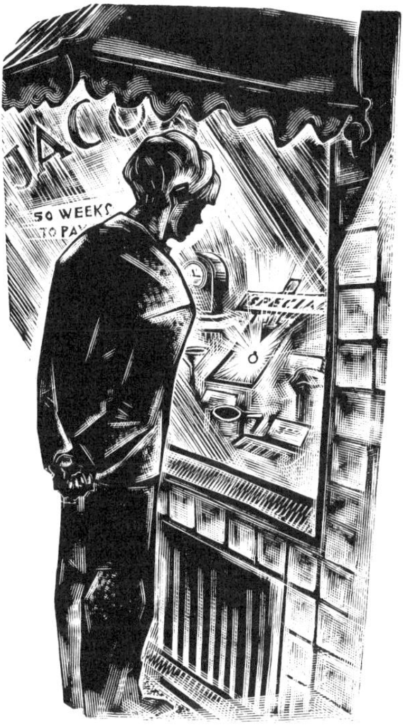

50 WEEKS
TO PAY
SPECIAL

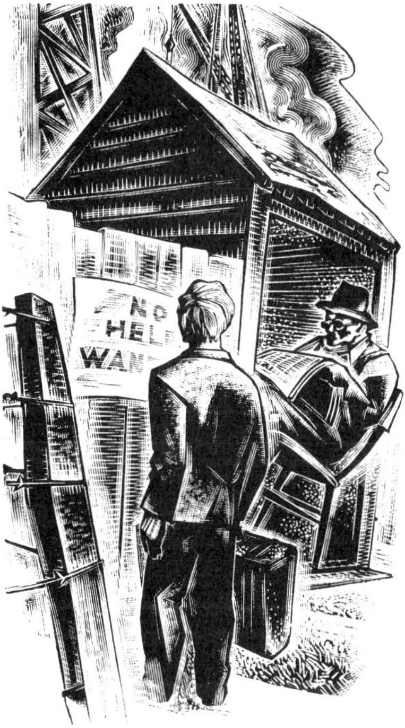
NO
HEL
WAN

MONDAY

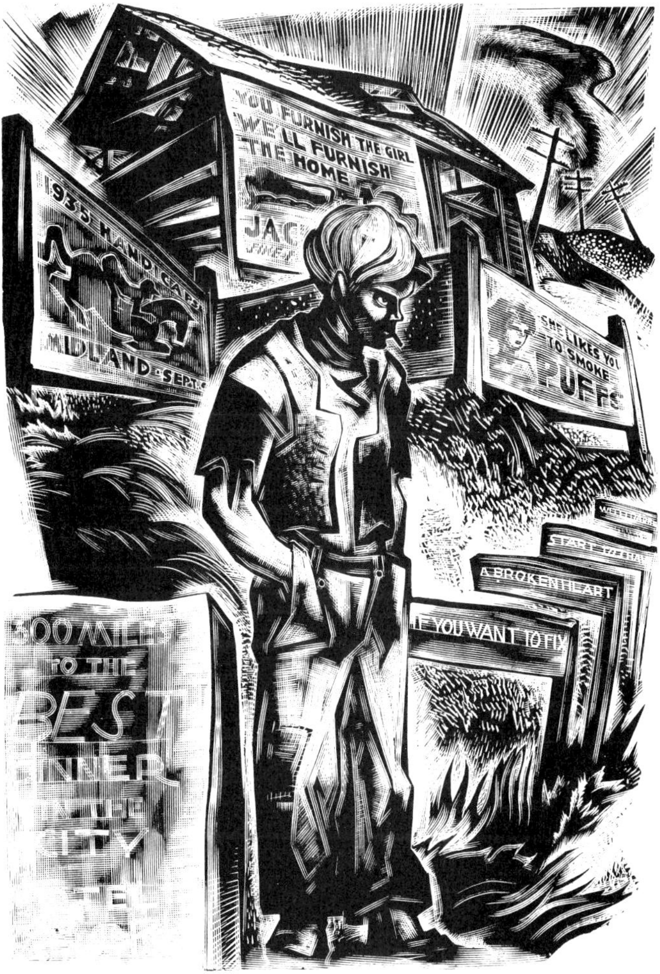
YOU FURNISH THE GIRL
WE LL FURNISH
THE HOME
JAC
1935 HANDICAPS
IDLAND-SEPT.
SHE LIKES YOU
TO SMOKE
PUFFS
A BROKEN HEART
IF YOU WANT TO FIX
300 MILES
TO THE
BEST
INNER
CITY

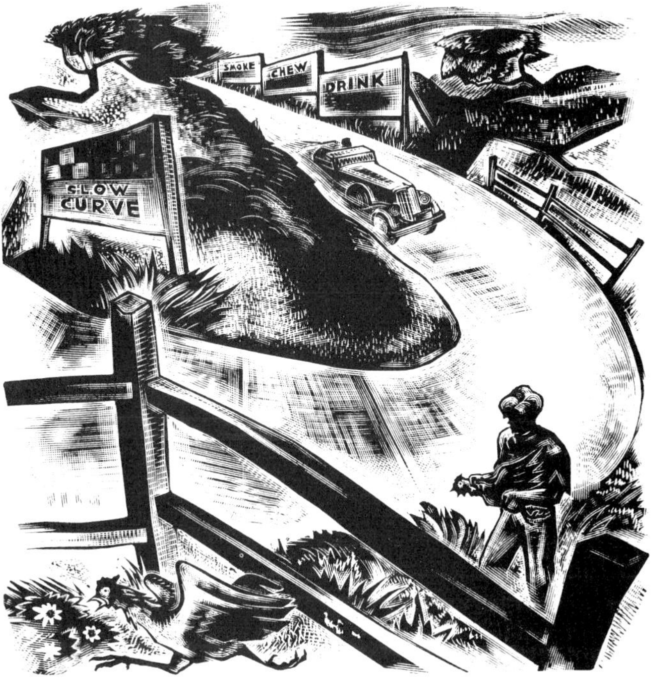
SMOKE
CHEW
DRINK
SLOW
CURVE

TUESDAY

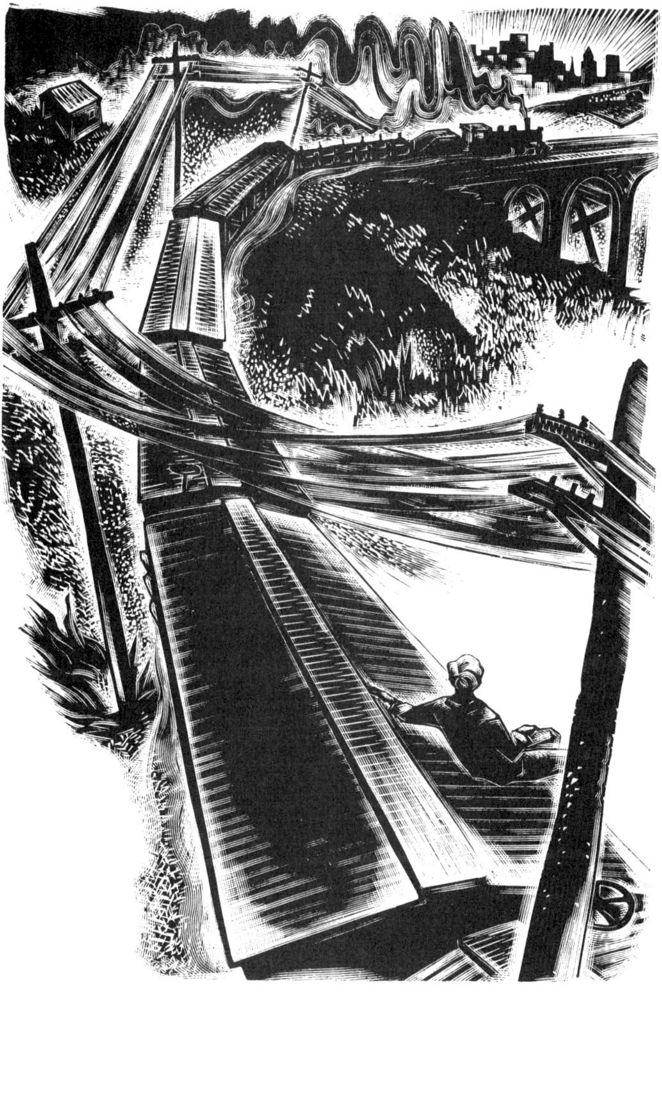

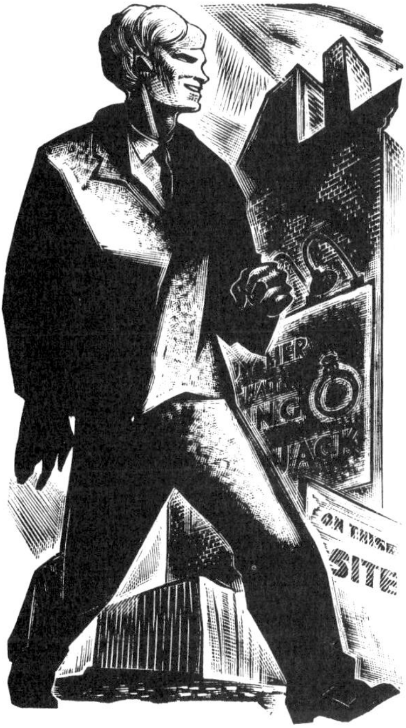
JACK
SITE

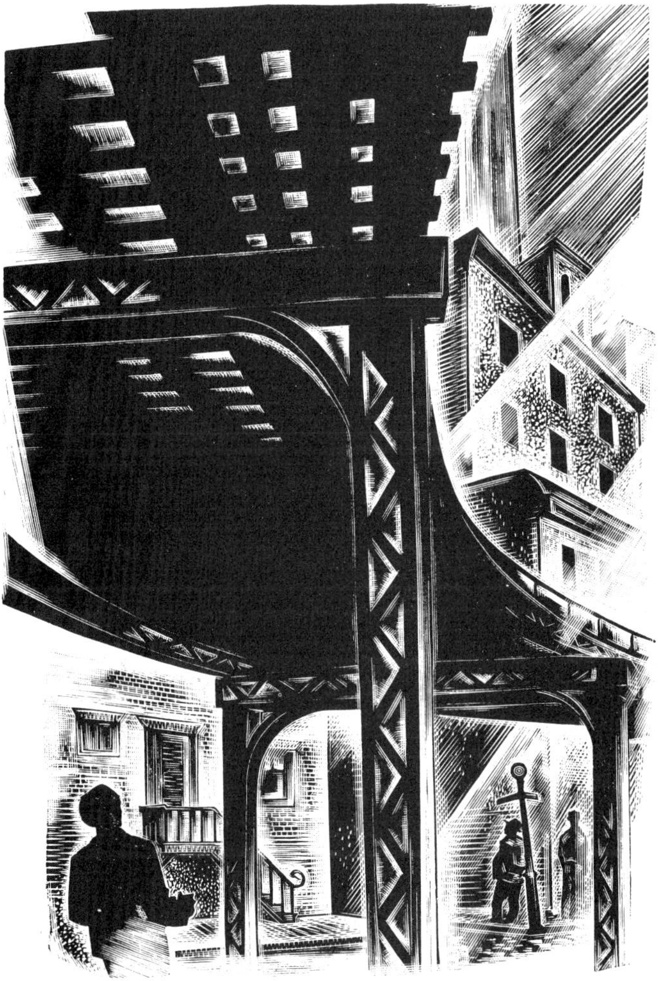

WEDNESDAY

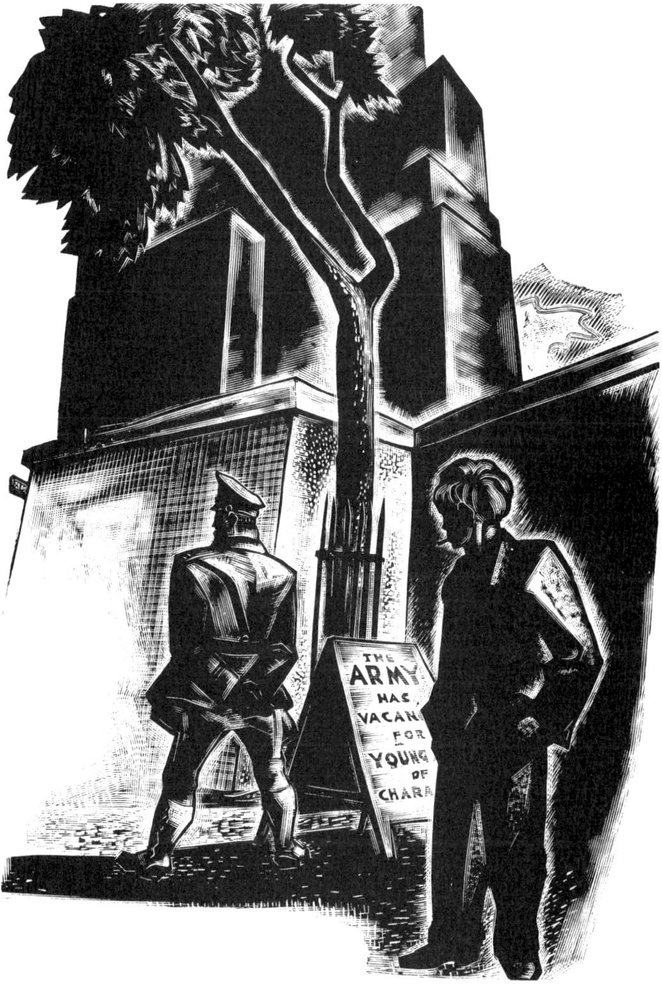
THE
ARMY
HAS
VACAN
FOR
YOUNG
OF
CHARA

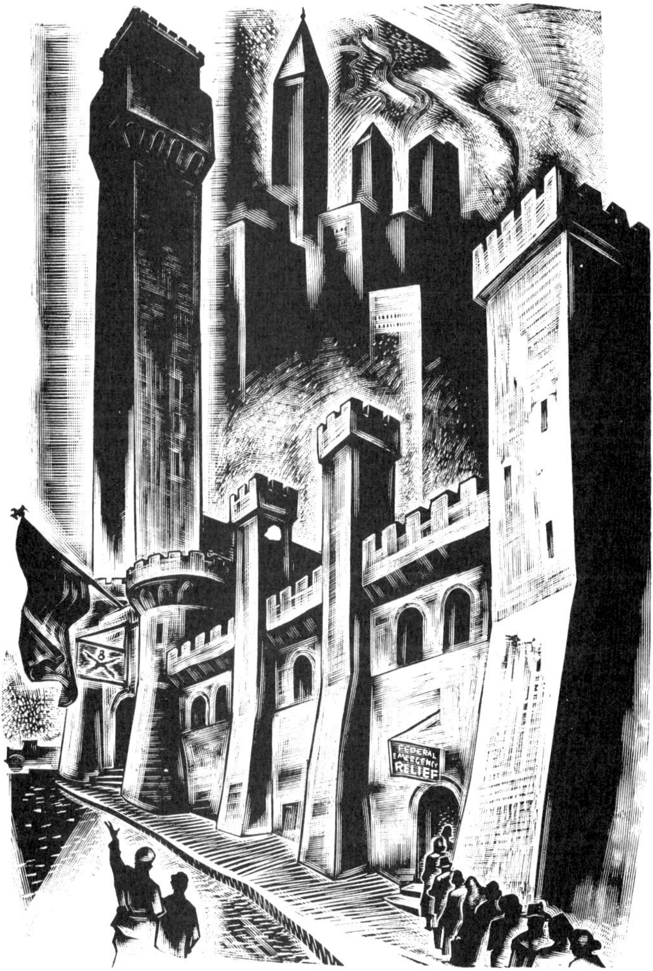
FEDERAL
EMERGENCY
RELIEF

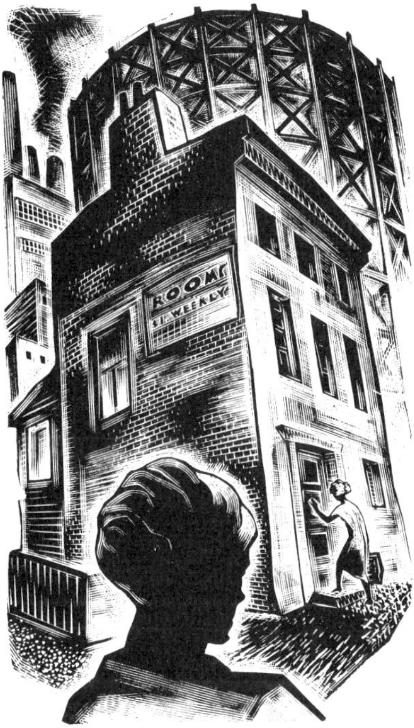
ROOMS
$1. WEEKLY

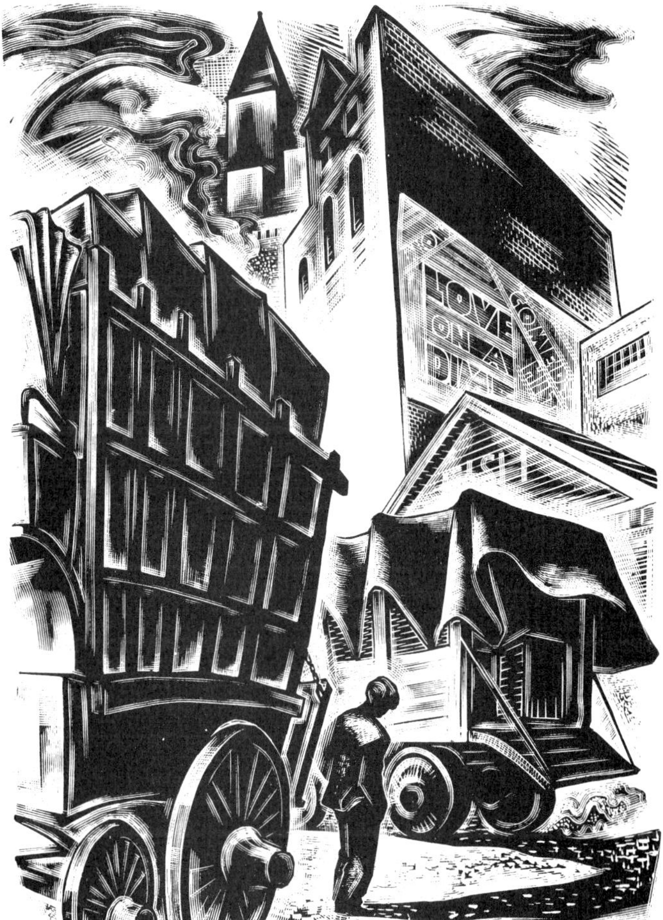
LOVE
ON A

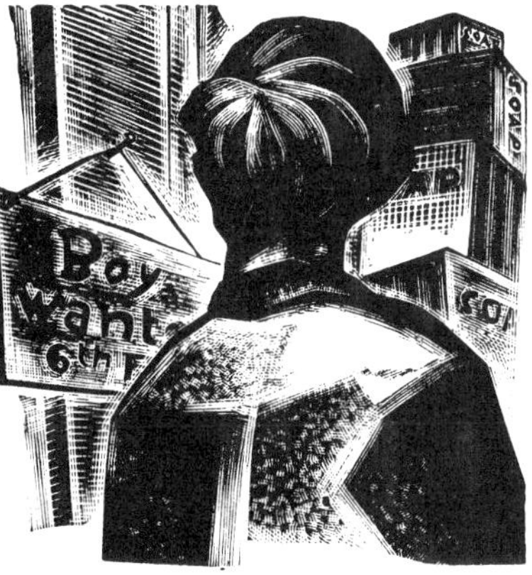
Boy
Want
6th

THURSDAY

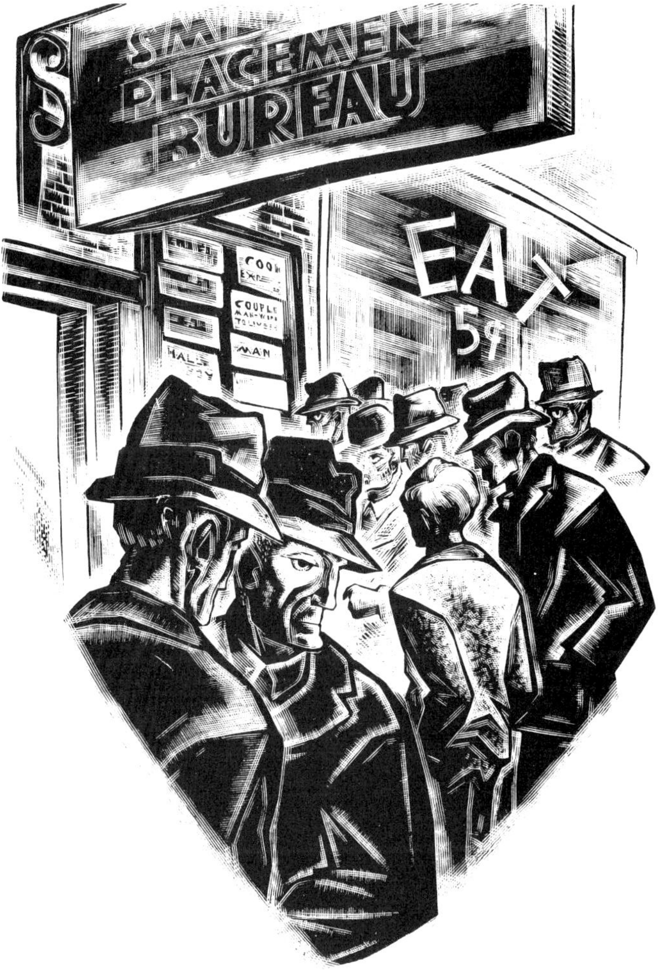
PLACEMENT
BUREAU
EAT
5¢
COUPLE
MAN

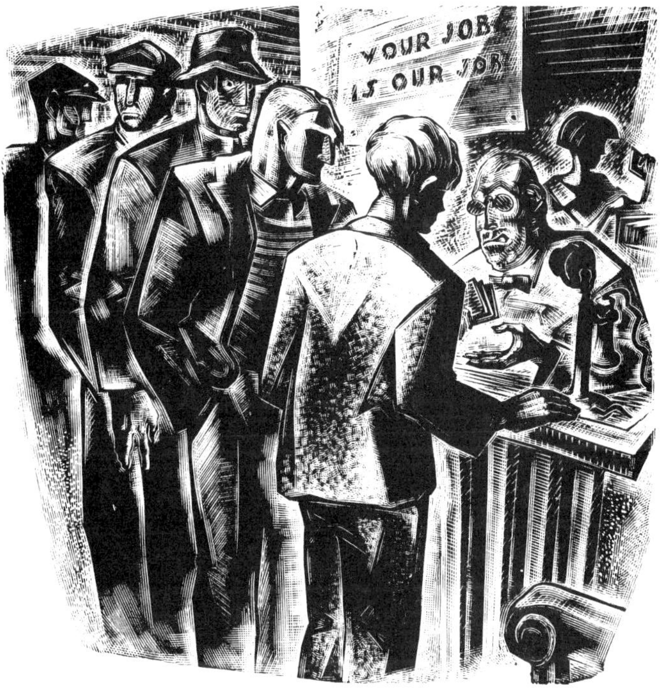
YOUR JOB
IS OUR JOB

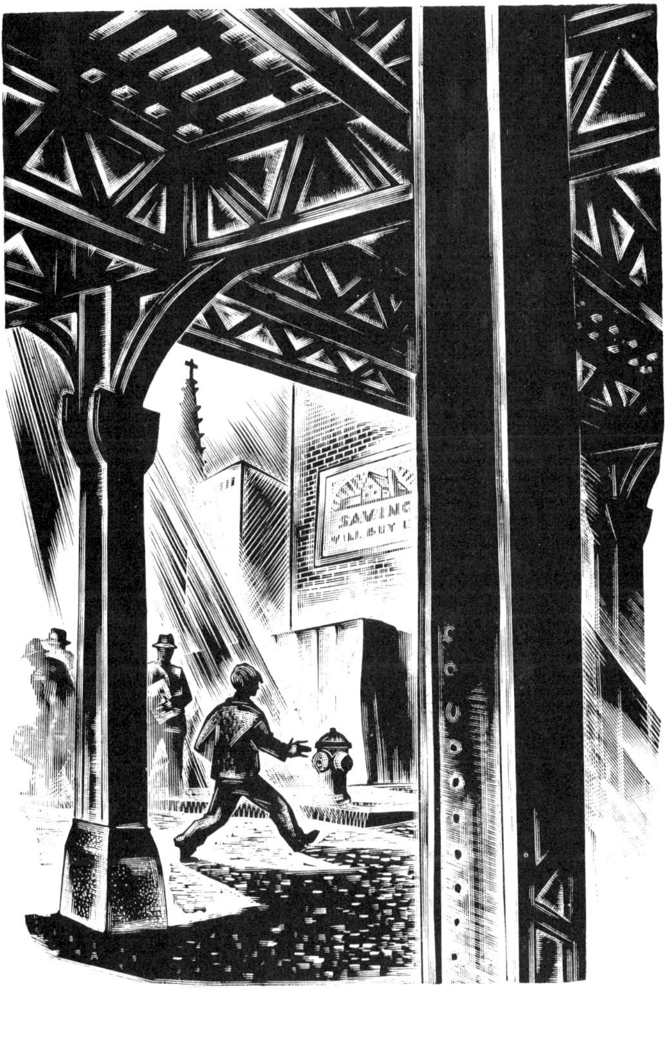

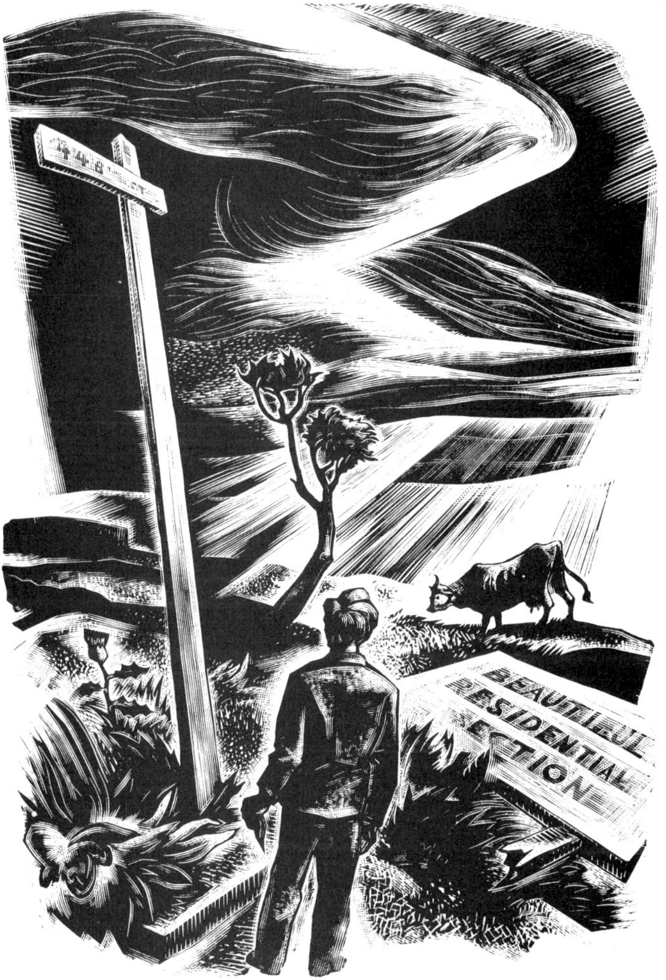
BEAUTIFUL
RESIDENTIAL
ECTION

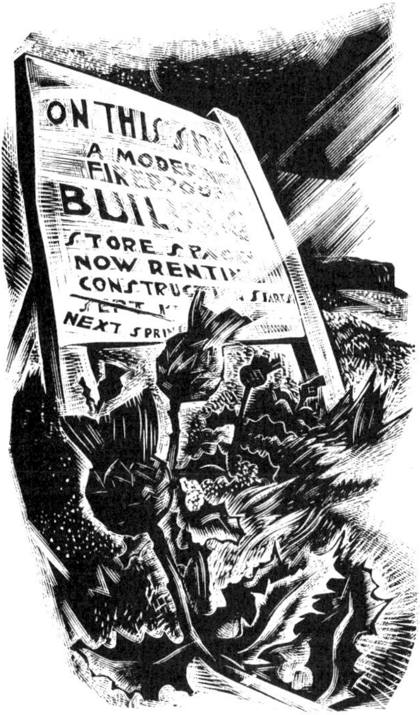
ON THIS
A MODES
BUIL
STORE SPA
NOW RENTI
CONSTRUC
NEXT SPRI

FRIDAY

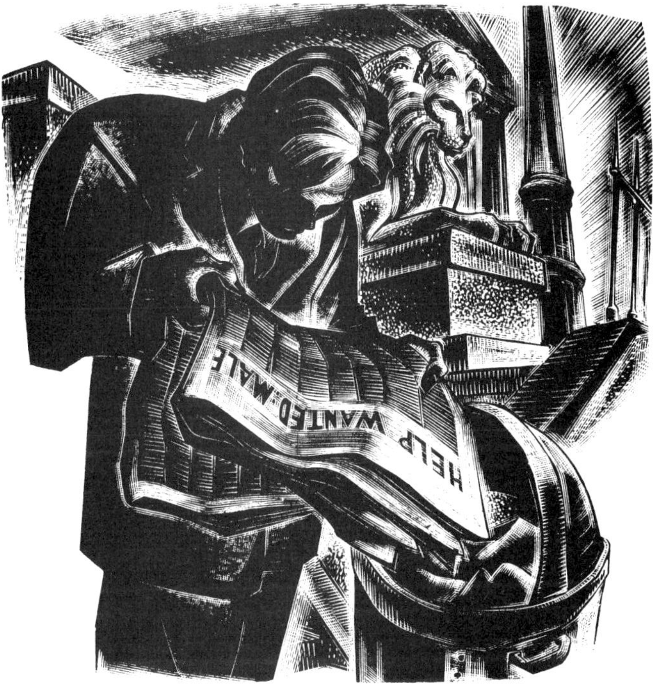
HELP WANTED-MALE

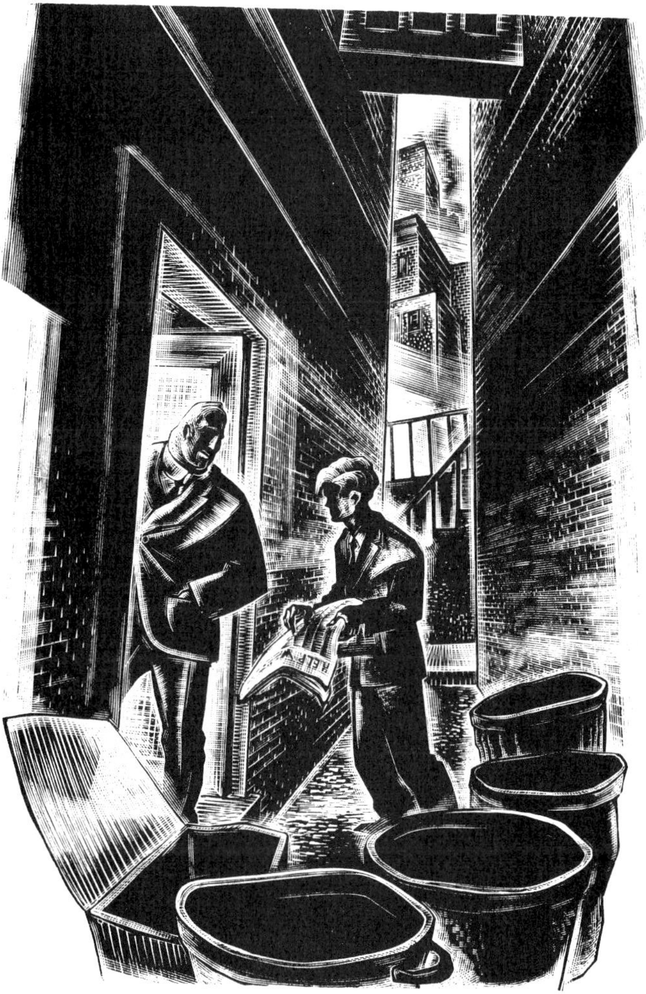

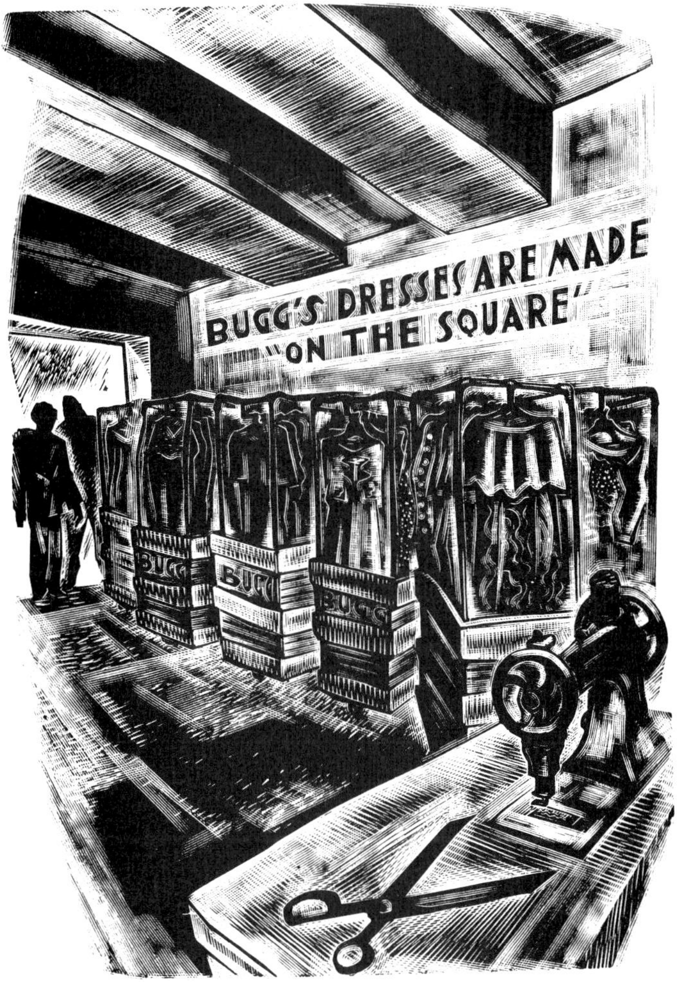
BUGG'S DRESSES ARE MADE
"ON THE SQUARE"
BUGG
BUGG
BUGG

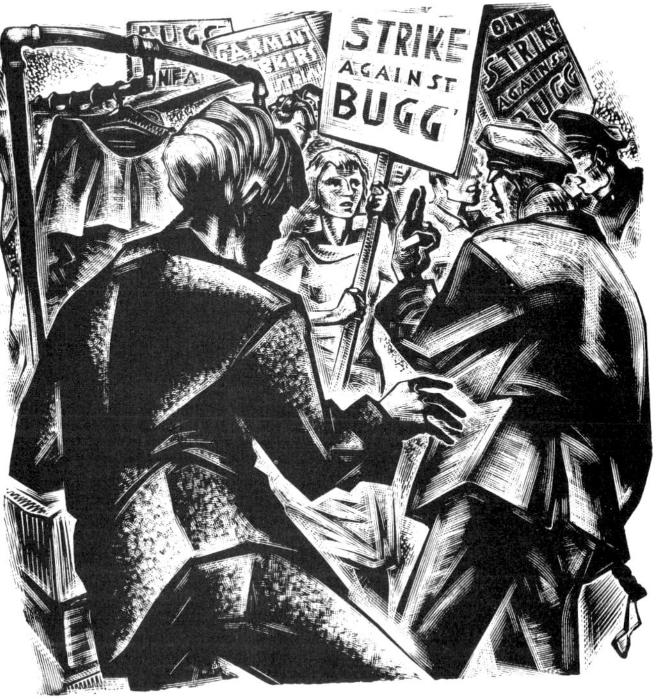
STRIKE
AGAINST
BUGG
GARMENT

SATURDAY

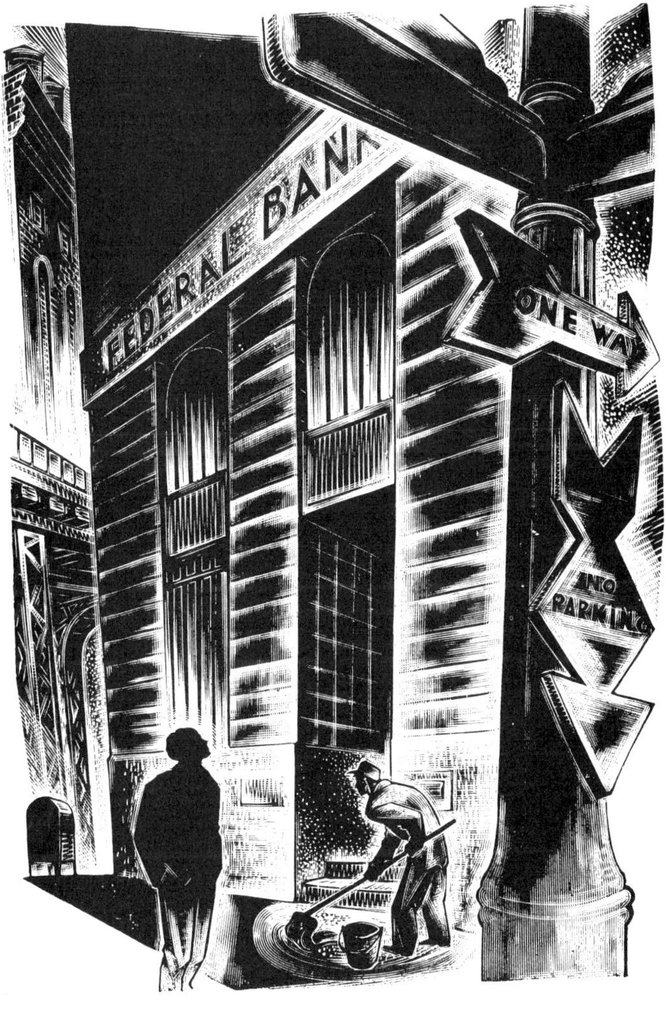
FEDERAL BANK
ONE WA
NO
PARKING

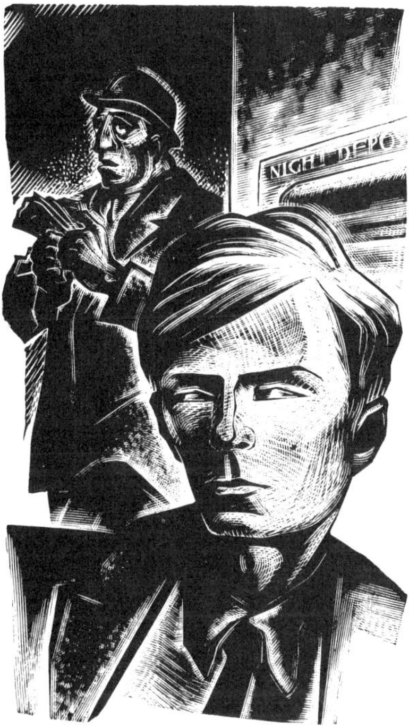
NIGHT DEPO

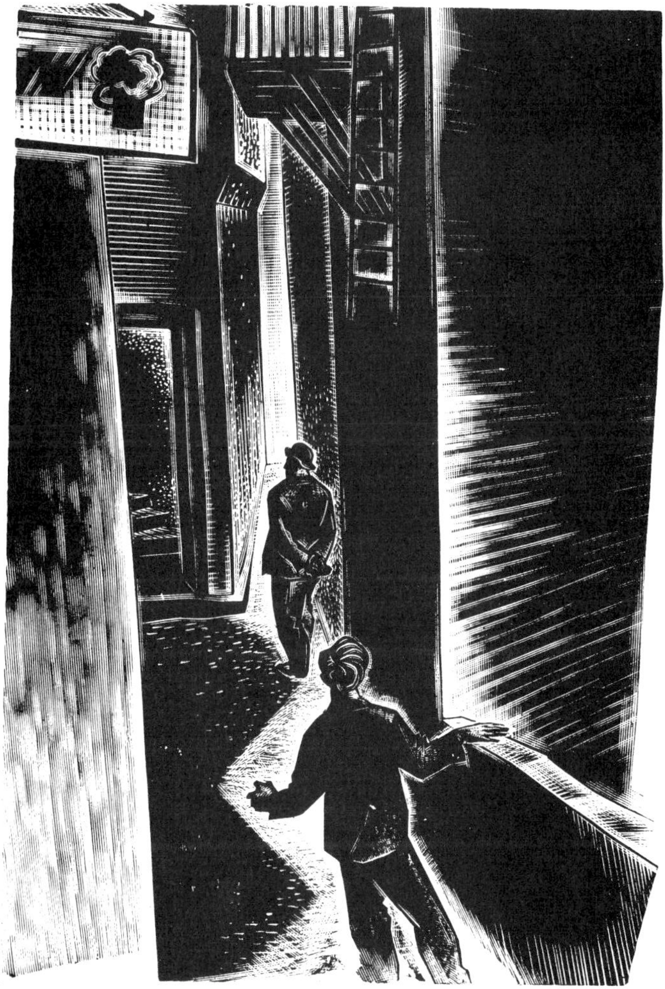

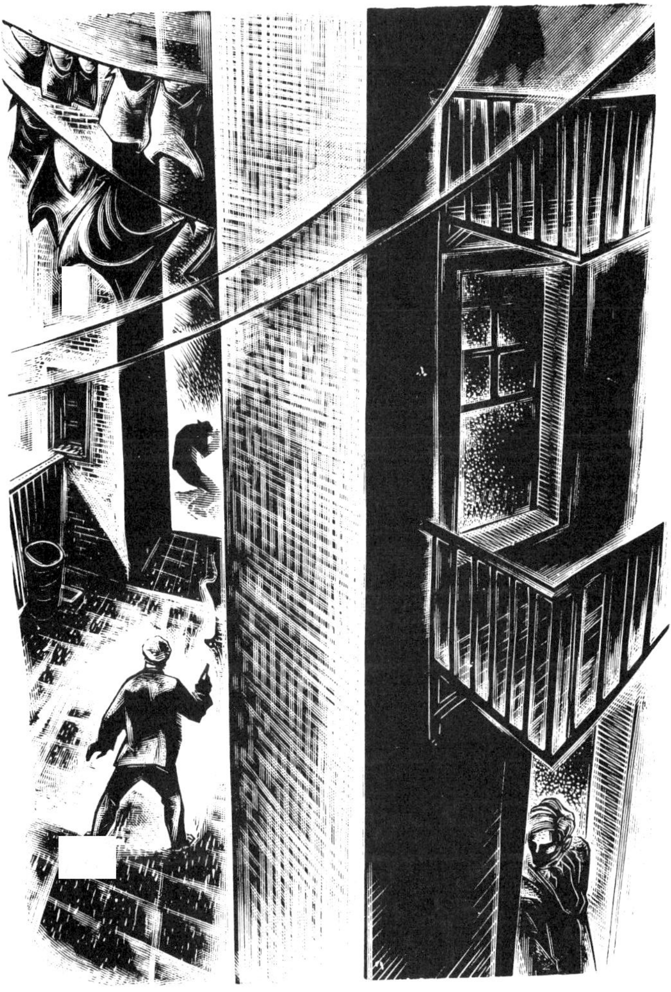

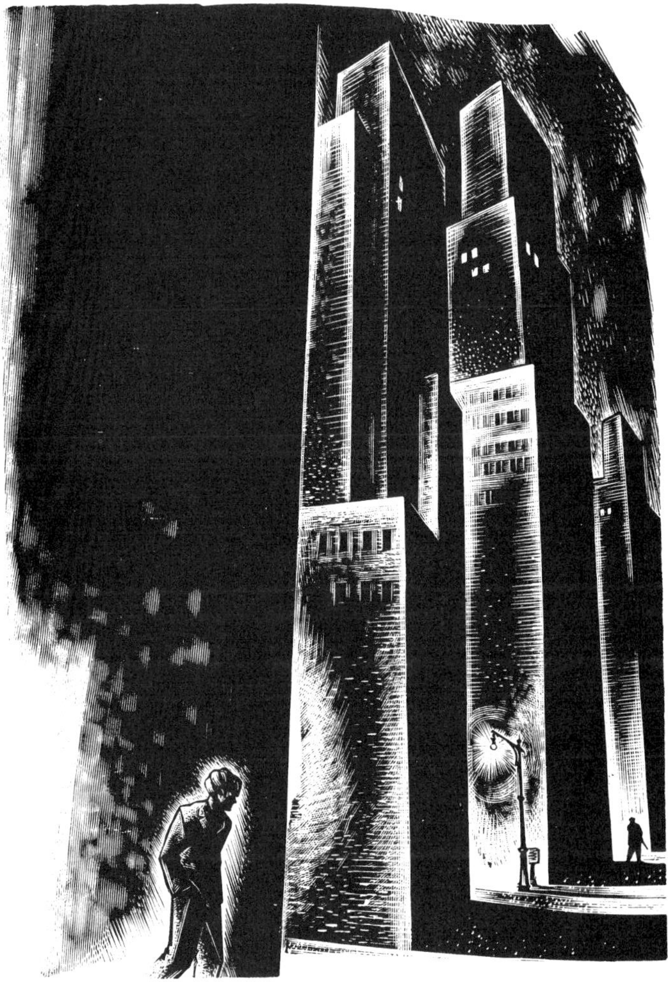

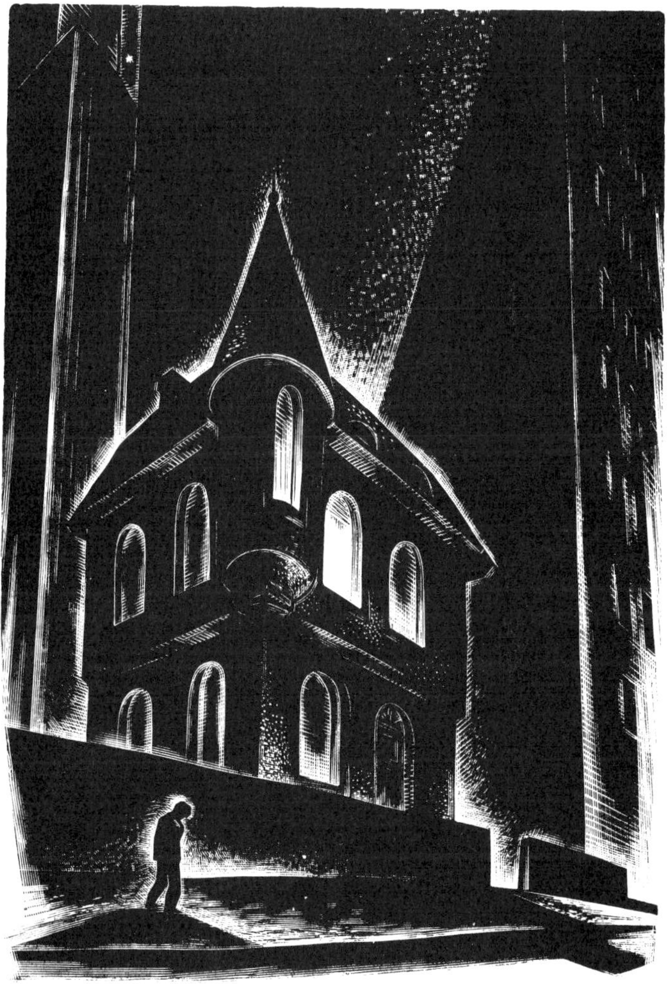

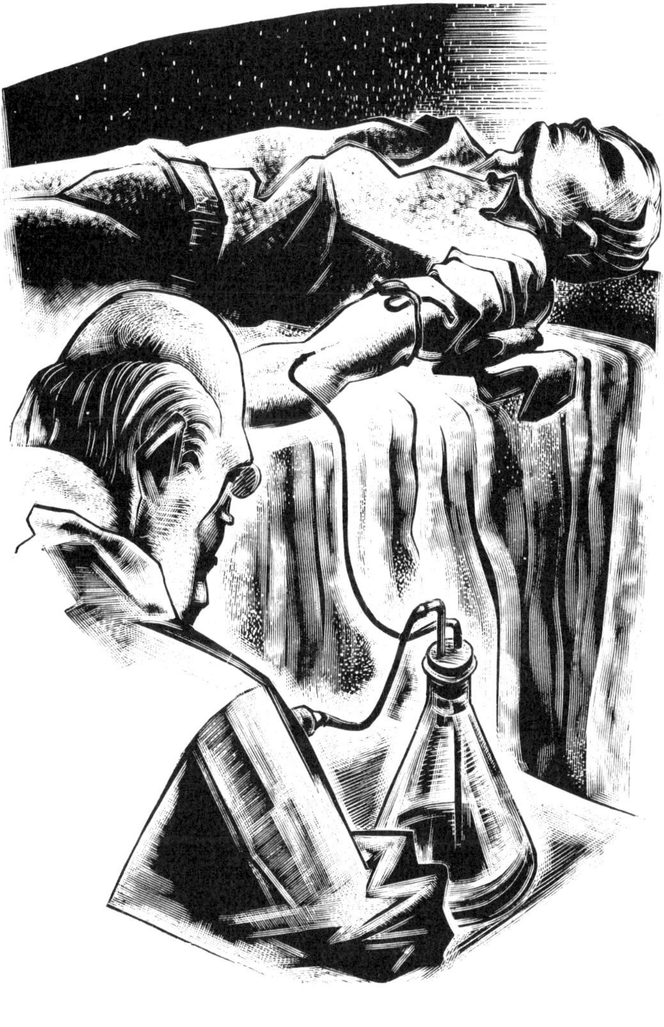

SUNDAY

ESSAYS

ON "PRELUDE TO A
MILLION YEARS"

I REMEMBER ONCE, when I was still young enough to regard the life of an artist as somehow special and endowed with magic and romance, I paid a visit to the studio of a well-known painter. He was a man with a national reputation, a long list of prizes, and was well established with one of the more prestigious galleries. The address I had took me to a remote corner of Greenwich Village and to an iron gate that opened on a narrow alleyway crowded with garbage cans. As a setting in which to find an artist, however, this did not seem completely inappropriate, for the air was filled with the strains of a Strauss waltz which I quickly identified as "Artists' Life."

As I climbed the rickety iron steps to the painter's door I realized that the music came from the back room of a hole-in-the-wall restaurant and that the steps were rusty to the point of being hazardous. Inside I found a half-finished painting of a basket of apples on an easel, and the painter huddled on a narrow cot with a blanket around his shoulders. The fruit basket on his work table contained only apple cores and was surrounded by the bottles of pills with which he was treating a cold contracted, as he explained, when his heat had been turned off by the landlord for nonpayment of rent. He hastened to assure me that he had only five more canvases to complete for his next show, which was coming up soon and would solve all his problems. As a matter of fact, when held, the exhibition resulted in only more unpaid bills, for these were the early years of the Depression.

Thus there were still some artists living in ivory towers, still totally immersed in the never-solved problems of an essentially private aesthetic, and still able to ignore the tremors that were moving in successive shock waves across the country and shaking the foundations of philosophic systems as well as of corporate structures. And there were still persons in all walks of life, many in positions of influence, who were stubbornly oblivious to what was happening. They continued to insist that the whole problem was psychological; all that was needed was a return of confidence, and the way to get that was to insist that everything was coming out all right.

In the art world there were some who welcomed this soporific interpretation of the crisis and argued that since most artists live close to a subsistence level anyway, the new problem was not really a great contrast to the problems they had had to cope with in the past. In this view, artists were relatively better off than those in other lines of work whose past experience of comfort made it more difficult for them to adjust to economic adversity and social insecurity.

But as time went on it became increasingly difficult for

artists to remain aloof and unaffected. Freelance commercial artists discovered that the "free" meant "free to starve," and even high-salaried art directors found themselves standing in line for a meager relief check, right behind the painter of the back-alley studio whose one-man show had somehow failed to solve his problems.

Our daily fare in those years, served up with scare headlines every morning, was a never-ending story of strikes, lay-offs, lock-outs, demonstrations, counter-demonstrations, and parades, all interlarded with polemical speeches. Inevitably a process of polarization of the citizenry was set in motion, and no one who simply undertook to walk across the city or venture into the nearby countryside could remain completely ignorant of what was happening to people, or completely unaffected by the changes occurring in the public temper.

During these months a question kept nudging me and eventually would not be suppressed. That question was simply whether, in the few years since a bundle of ideas about the place of the artist in the modern world had coalesced into the story *Gods' Man*, the social setting had not changed so completely that it would be reasonable to update the action.

This consideration brought me to a point where the inner movie machine began whirring again, focusing this time on a sculptor rather than a painter, but in the end, and by design, resulting in a far shorter sequence than any of the earlier books.

I have always thought of *Prelude to a Million Years* as a kind of footnote to *Gods' Man*, a sort of codicil that would acknowledge that changes had occurred and that these changes required an amendment to the earlier testament. It was a very limited statement, running to a total of only thirty blocks. Because it was a minor work it was printed directly from the woodblocks on a beautiful rag paper in a small edition. *Prelude* was the third publication of Equinox Cooperative Press, a group of young people, including myself, working in printing, publishing, and the book arts who wanted to do non-commercial books, just for the love of doing it. Each copy of *Prelude* was bound by hand and made with loving care.

THE EQUINOX IDEA

FLYING IN THE FACE of the current wisdom that warned of the foolishness of starting any new enterprise in a time of pervasive economic stagnation, let alone a book-publishing enterprise, I began in the early thirties to talk with friends about precisely that: a small undertaking to produce a few books a year that would be different from those coming off the big presses. The books would involve us directly in as many of the basic operations of book production as possible.

Several of those who responded to the challenge of this proposal were individuals currently employed in commercial publishing. The others shared my own overriding enthusiasm for books as a unique cultural phenomenon and brought to the group talents of one sort or another that were indispensable to the variety of functions we were preparing to undertake.

American publishing at this time was far from being the mechanized conglomerate it was later to become. But it was enough of a prisoner of its cog wheels and cost counting to make many of the young people, who worked in the back rooms where routine is master, end up with the feeling that they were missing out on the most important aspects of publishing. My friends, then, were ready for the Equinox idea.

What this meant was a return to basics. What that meant was a reaffirmation of handiwork, a somewhat mystical belief that to touch directly the materials and processes of the making of a book would result in a better book. It was, in a sense, an extension into the twentieth century of that ancient Greek myth wherein the giant Antæus defeated all opponents because every time he touched the earth he gained fresh strength.

Our sources of strength were, over the years, to involve us in setting type, folding printed sheets, producing printable images on wood and stone without dependence on photomechanical processes, and stenciling binding designs directly on the boards. Unlike most small presses that so often depend on the public domain to provide textual material, Equinox from the beginning placed great emphasis on the words whose dissemination all this handwork was dedicated to serve.

Over the years the importance of the word increased, not through any design on the part of any members, but, I tend to think, as a result of the pressure of events in the world around. The economic difficulties of the early thirties were gradually overshadowed in the late thirties by a horizon dark with the ominous clouds of war—from Spain on. The question of what words Equinox should be working with became increasingly hard to define.

In all its decisions, Equinox was guided by a belief in

the democratic process. The discussions of every basic point were wide-ranging, always completely frank, and often interminable. But the very structure of the organization was an assertion of the necessity of democratic relationships in all aspects of life. In seeking a corporate form that would reflect this belief in the democratic way, we decided to organize as a cooperative. But we discovered that the laws governing cooperatives were sharply defined, with consumer cooperatives on the one side and producer cooperatives on the other. Since we were producers, we were incorporated as a producer cooperative. But since most producers are, in the nature of things, farmers, we became the only publishers in the history of Western culture who had to file annual reports with the New York State Department of Agriculture.

However effective official documents such as annual reports may be in providing statistics about the workings of the farms of the Empire State, I'm sure our reports on the workings of a small group of disenchanted idealists failed to convey that we felt it was important that that handful of books (you can carry the entire production of Equinox in two armfuls) be given the permanency the making of a book achieves. None of us has entirely the same feeling about every book. I end up with the realization that none of the dozen or so says eloquently or persuasively that it is the book I wanted to come from my involvement with the Equinox Press. But beyond the work we all did together, there is a realization that what we all learned about the world and about each other were the things no annual report will ever find a way to measure.

ON "SONG WITHOUT WORDS"

I HAVE ALWAYS held that the individual who "reads" a pictorial narrative should feel completely free to develop his own interpretation and end up with something that is right for him. The cumulative associations of his own experience will provide a basis for understanding and endow each image encountered with significance or meaning. But if the reader's relation to the world has been markedly different from that of the artist who created the pictorial sequence, there will be little common ground between them. This may well result in a feeling of bafflement, for inevitably a reader wants to feel that he understands what is being said. This problem, if problem it be, is not unique to pictorial narrative, for it is a feeling occasionally shared, I understand, by readers of contemporary fiction as well as by theater- and gallery-goers.

However, if the reader perseveres he may very well arrive at an interpretation quite different from the intention that generated the narrative. Or he may perceive more in the images than was consciously put in by the creator. But his reading is not thereby any less valid.

That this possibility is inherent in the medium was brought home to me most vividly when a doctor friend, to whom I had given a copy of *Song Without Words*, explained in detail how, after a period of early confusion, he had been able to follow the course of the action easily and with full comprehension as soon as he realized that a particular block represented the beginning of morning sickness, the next one nausea and vomiting, the one after that backache and dizziness, and so on through a very clinical nine months. (The only thing he seemed to have missed was insemination.) Needless to say, his specialty was obstetrics. It is true that pregnancy was very much a part of the basic concepts that make up this sequence. But from my point of view, it represented more than just that.

By the summer of 1936 it was impossible for anyone, artist or not, to remain ignorant of the fact that the world was in trouble and that the trouble seemed to be getting worse. Panaceas were a dime a dozen, but every dose of medicine seemed only to aggravate the situation. For almost everyone the day-to-day struggle was simply with the problems of getting by—of paying enough of the rent to keep the landlord from throwing you out on the street or keeping the mortgage from being foreclosed, of having a few dollars for the weekly grocery budget, fewer dollars for clothing, and for extras, nothing at all.

But looming larger on everyone's horizon was the ominous shadow of Fascism, and for that no one had a panacea. Or more to the point, no one had a preventive serum. National boundaries proved no barrier to the spread of what seemed with each new day to be a lethal infection whose invasion no body politic could withstand. The awareness of what Mussolini had done to Italy was reinforced by the record of what had happened in Japan and by what Hitler was doing to Germany. The fate of Spain was an object lesson in how Fascist ideology could make a mockery of democratic institutions. Fascism threatened every believer in democratic freedoms, for the heart of the problem seemed to be that its supporters were to be found in every nation, and fascists everywhere were ready to supply both ideological support and the materiel for warfare. The ominous prospect was of successive assaults on one democratic government after another.

In this extremity it was probably not surprising that the most sensitive and concerned young people seriously questioned what future they could look forward to and what would be the substance of their remaining years. Many also questioned the morality and wisdom of bringing children into a world that had already proved how many hazards it could provide for the newborn—how many varied fates it held in store for those who had the audacity to survive babyhood.

In *Song Without Words* I tried to work out a sequence of images that, if not an answer to the questioning, would at least say something about the need for faith. When finished it was only twenty-one blocks long, and I have never thought of it as a story. The nearest I can come to identifying it is to say that if a sequence of images could be called prose, this could be considered a kind of prose poem. Because this was again a minor work, it was printed directly from the blocks in a small edition.

ON "VERTIGO"

I sometimes wonder how many of those who live in this great metropolitan area remember, as they drive along Manhattan's West Side Highway and make the swing at Seventy-second Street to the elevated structure that carries the roadway on down between the city's docks and warehouses, that in that spot in the early thirties there was a Hooverville—a sprawling complex of shanties spread over many acres, built of junk from the city's dumps. In that incredible labyrinth of strangely ordered refuse lived a small army of the homeless and the unemployed, victims of the pervasive economic slowdown that produced such shanty towns all across the land. The contrast between this symbol of hopelessness and the mansions and high-rise apartments that overlooked it from Riverside Drive was too insistent to be denied. It was a contrast that seemed almost unreal but that nevertheless constituted one of the great realities of the Depression.

In recent years there has been an increasing concern with that period of our past. It seems to reflect, particularly in the younger generations, a desire to know something about what happened and to understand why it happened. This strikes a responsive chord in those of us who lived through it, for while at the time we knew pretty well what happened, there were and still are large elements of mystery as to *why*.

During the thirties there were very few people, whether artists or not, who could remain uninvolved, either on a direct personal level or indirectly as human beings of conscience. It seemed that only the morally crippled or the socially irresponsible could fail to react to the obvious effect that vast, complicated, and impersonal social forces were having on the substance of so many individual lives.

For artists, especially, those years inevitably brought a multitude of experiences which were thrown up by the turmoil of the surrounding situation. Without consciously looking or listening, our eyes and ears were filled with sights and sounds that accumulated day by day, were measured, sorted, rearranged, and stitched together to achieve a new significance that finally demanded some release in work.

But there was a fundamental question of how so complex a mass of experiences could be given a form that would be manageable from the point of view of pictorial narrative and intelligible from the point of view of a reader. In many ways this problem of basic composition was more difficult for *Vertigo* than for any of my other books.

It was obvious that apart from the symbolic figure wearing a label that a cartoonist uses by way of personification, it is impossible to establish a satisfactory single image that will convey the essence of what we mean by "impersonal social force." At the same time it is difficult for a reader to feel very much identification with a crowd; it is with a single human being, whether victim or hero, that we become emotionally involved. These considerations led me to conclude that what I wanted to say might be expressed by using several individual figures whose lives and backgrounds would be stated individually in turn, but the events of whose lives would be so intertwined—so much a matter of action, reaction, and interaction—that a totality would result in which the impersonal would be implied in purely personal terms. It might even be possible to suggest that an impersonal social force is the accumulation of individual actions for which individuals are finally responsible.

This book proved to be the longest of all, not only because of its more complicated story but because I was anxious to make as explicit a statement as possible. To accomplish that I broke down the action into many small steps, using several small blocks to bring the reader in close to a character so that facial expression would register more effectively the emotional response of that character to what was happening, thereby involving the reader's own emotions more completely.

And in order to provide the reader with a structure, I divided the book into three sections, each identified with one of the three persons whose individual stories make up the whole. These sections are in turn subdivided into units of time that become progressively shorter as the book moves along, starting with years, going on to months, and ending up with days. If this treatment of time seems to suggest that somehow time itself moves faster as we get older, it was not consciously intended: but if this interpretation helps anyone to understand the work I would not dispute it. (However, my own involvement with the story would suggest the opposite, for it took much longer to finish this book than any of its predecessors, requiring the best part of two years.)

The book was published under the title of *Vertigo*, which was meant to suggest that the illogic of what we saw happening all around us in the thirties was enough to set the mind spinning through space and the emotions hurtling from great hope to the depths of despair.

THE BOOK
AND THE WOODBLOCK

To anyone who has been impressed by the frequency with which books over the years have been illustrated with woodcuts or wood engravings, it will come as no surprise to find that this relationship has its roots in a historical affinity that goes back many centuries. In fact, the most sober of scholars might find it difficult to say which owes more to the other. Could the printed book have been developed if there had not been in existence a body of knowledge and a fund of experience derived from the printing of woodblocks? And, conversely, without the book, might not the woodblock have remained only the prosaic duplicator of textile designs, playing cards, and religious souvenirs for which it was originally used?

In any event, there was a time in fifteenth-century Europe when a burst of inventive energy resulted in the development of movable type and at the same time necessitated the use of woodblocks to provide pictures that could be printed directly on the book page along with the type. Looking back from this distance, it is hard for us to realize how heretical this new way of producing images then seemed, and those who designed and cut woodblocks found life difficult. Along with the problems inherent in their craft, they had to fight the bitter opposition of the guilds of scribes and illuminators, which were very successful in having it declared illegal to duplicate images by any means save the hand of the scribe or illuminator. Thus for some years the woodcutter worked like a forger, adding color tints to deceive the unwary into thinking the printed picture was a drawing. Not until a press was installed in the Sorbonne itself were the barriers broken down. Then the way gradually opened for a forthright collaboration between the printer of books and the cutter of blocks. The subsequent list of volumes that bear witness to the rich harvest of this joint labor is a long one.

Although those early years of printing produced much that has since been acknowledged as masterful in design and execution, printed books were for some time regarded as second class in comparison with those done by hand, and great patrons of the arts were ashamed to have printed books on the shelves of their libraries.

In this as in so many areas of human affairs, there was a gradual erosion of prejudice until printed books illustrated with woodblocks came to be accepted. At first completely anonymous and hence unknown to us, the woodblock artists who worked on books came in time to include persons of the stature of Michael Wohlgemut, Lucas Cranach the Elder, and Albrecht Dürer. But with time the need for specialization also developed, and the specialists turned out to be craftsmen who were in no sense creators themselves. They were highly skilled artisans whose knife and gouge could cut in wood anything that the artist drew on the block. All through history, it seems, the creative relation between artist and material has been too easily corrupted. The loss of personal contact with the block, plate, or stone that actually produces a print has again and again proved the undoing of all the graphic processes. One searches in vain for a recognition by later book illustrators of the need to be directly involved. Then, toward the end of the eighteenth century, it was reported that an engraver (who has never been identified) appeared in Paris claiming he had developed a way of using engraving tools on an end-grain block so that the resulting print was superior in fineness of line to any current work with knife and gouge. The woodcutters said he was mad, but this was in fact the technical development that made possible the re-establishment of a genuinely creative relationship between the artist and the woodblock.

That vital reaffirmation also manifested itself in the singular person of an Englishman named Thomas Bewick (1753–1828). Apprenticed to a copper-plate engraver, Bewick was obviously skilled in the technical requirements of handling gravers and took naturally to the use of such tools on an end-grain block. But endowed with a natural talent for drawing, and preferring to work on his own designs rather than to handle only the more mechanical rendering of decorative designs, he soon developed the natural potential of engraving tools on the end-grain block. This meant using the white line as the primary means of developing the subject. Bewick's great contribution was in the sensitive use of that line so as to define successfully complex subject matter—here narrow and finely drawn, there wider and stronger in emphasis. He developed special techniques for lowering the surface of the block when less pressure was required to produce especially delicate effects, and he trained printers in the procedures necessary to obtain the results he wanted.

But beyond that, Bewick trained other craftsmen in his way of working, and so it was not long before printing offices came into being where wood engravers were employed to produce printable images using the new techniques. From there it was but a step to the re-emergence of the craftsman—the wood engraver who could render in facsimile whatever the artist, working independently, could draw. The high point, or low point if you will, of this method of working was reached at the time of Gustave Doré (1833–1883), a Frenchman whose facility in drawing was exceeded only by the genuine strength of his interpretive capacities and the range of his imaginative response to literary works. He was a prolific worker, and though he died at fifty, he had illustrated well over a hundred books, ranging from Rabelais to the Bible. He is said to have kept more than a dozen engravers constantly at work, and in such a volume as *Don Quixote* it is possible to see the strength and weaknesses of the contemporary practice of wood engraving without which Doré's work in books would not have been possible.

The Book and the Woodblock

In *Don Quixote* two ways of working are easily distin-guished. For the headings and tailpieces, Doré drew on the block with a pen line, and the engraver merely cut away the wood between the lines. The result preserves all the spontaneity and lively quality of the original. For the full pages, however, the drawing was made in wash on the surface of a block lightly coated with Chinese white. The task of the engraver, then, was to cut an infinite number of wavy parallel lines, here wider, there narrower, that when printed would produce an effect of gray, and to render the figures and background landscape in the variety of tones of the original wash drawing. In thus being able to render with impartiality any and all parts of the subject of the block, wood engraving laid itself open for the lethal blow that the camera and photomechanical methods of reproduction were preparing to give it.

Today, the far greater technical competence of photo-graphic reproductive processes has made the use of wood-blocks in books obsolete, except to the extent that they can provide a graphic quality obtainable in no other way. For example, wood engraving can give something to a set of illustrations for *Frankenstein* that is somehow differ-ent from the result that would be produced by the same pictures in watercolor, or lithographs, or line drawings. If what is different contributes to a mood that is right for the story being illustrated, then that is the justification—and the only justification—for working in wood engrav-ing. And as long as that ability to contribute something of value remains, wood engraving will endure.

CHRONOLOGY

NOTE ON THE TEXTS

NOTES

CHRONOLOGY

1905   Born Lynd Kendall Ward, June 26, in Chicago, Illinois, the second child of Harry Frederick Ward (b. Chiswick, England, 1873) and Harriet May "Daisy" Kendall Ward (b. Kansas City, Mo., 1873). (Father was a devout Methodist who left England for America in 1891, inspired by the American religious and economic reformer Richard T. Ely's message, articulated in his *Social Aspects of Christianity*, 1889, that "Christianity is primarily concerned with *this* world, and it is the mission of Christianity to bring to pass here a kingdom of righteousness and redeem all our social relations." He studied philosophy and economics at the University of Southern California–Los Angeles, Northwestern University, and Harvard; his teachers included George Albert Coe, Francis Peabody, and William James. By 1905 he was an elder of the Union Avenue Methodist Episcopal Church and head resident of the Northwestern University Settlement House, which like Jane Addams's Hull House was an engine of social reform in "Progressive Era" Chicago. He and Daisy Kendall, who met as undergraduates at Northwestern, were married in April 1899; their first child, Gordon Hugh Ward, was born in June 1903.) Father chooses name "Lynd" as an allusion to Lyndhurst, the village in the New Forest where, in his early teens, he spent two years recovering from rheumatic fever and developed a reverence for nature and a love of camping, fishing, and cabin-building. Infant Lynd, born healthy, soon contracts tuberculosis in the "back-of-the-yards" miasma of the settlement-house neighborhood; he is taken by parents to their summer retreat on Lonely Lake, thirty miles northeast of Sault Ste. Marie, Ontario, where from July through October he makes a partial recovery. Remains a sickly child throughout his early years, his abating tuberculosis complicated by acute inner-ear and mastoid infections.

1907   Sister, Muriel Ward, born February 18. In December, father and four other American Methodist churchmen, seeking to improve the lives of workers, form the Methodist Federation for Social Service (MFSS), a national organization dedicated to mobilizing clergy and laity to take action on issues of poverty and social injustice.

1908   In May, at the General Conference of the Methodist Episcopal Church in Washington, D.C., father presents his "Social Creed of the Churches," calling for the abolition of child labor, a shortened work week, greater workplace safety, and a living wage for all workers. Later that year, the "Social Creed" is adopted by the ecumenical Federal Council of Churches, and soon becomes synonymous with the moral argument for American workplace reform.

1909   To promote better health for Lynd and for himself, father moves family to suburban Oak Park, Illinois, and assumes pastorship of the Euclid Avenue Methodist Episcopal Church.

1911   Father founds the *Social Questions Bulletin*, the official organ of the MFSS, which he will edit (and, most issues, write) for the next thirty-four years. Lynd, now school-aged, shows a strong aptitude for drawing; he feels destined to become an artist when his first-grade teacher tells him that "Ward" is "draw" spelled backward.

1912   Bishop Francis John McConnell elected president of the MFSS and promotes father to director. Harry F. Ward becomes the public face of Methodist activism, preaching the Social Creed from coast to coast; during his first eighteen months under McConnell he delivers 347 lectures and leads thirty-six conferences in seventeen states. Lynd now seldom sees him except during summers, when the family takes its annual three-month vacation at the camp on Lonely Lake. Father's work-year absences make Lynd aware of "the tragic gulf between a man's professional success and the reality of his family life," while summers in Ontario make him equally aware of his own "close bond with the strength of the wilderness." During these summers, father teaches Lynd to fish and to hunt small game, and to do carpentry and stonework; he also encourages him to record his natural surroundings in words and pictures.

1913   In summer, Bishop McConnell secures father part-time professorship in Social Service at the Boston University School of Theology; the MFSS office moves to the BU campus and the Ward family to suburban Newton Centre, Massachusetts. Lynd enters third grade at Mason Grammar School (K–8), the local public elementary school.

1915   At age ten Lynd is a bookish child, fascinated by children's picture books and by the engravings in the family's copy of *Doré's Gallery of Bible Illustrations* (1891). By studying and copying them, he later recalled, "I was learning, without realizing it, what makes the book a unique form of expression. . . . For the artist, the turning of the page is the thing he has that no other worker in the visual arts has: the power to control a succession of images in time." Mother encourages his interest in art by planning regular outings to Boston's many art museums. Lynd also learns to play the family piano, mainly by ear; his repertoire is Methodist hymns, folk songs, and popular songs of his parents' era.

1918   On June 21, Ward, having skipped a grade, graduates from Mason Grammar School at age twelve. Father accepts appointment as director of the Department of Christian Ethics at Union Theological Seminary, New York City, and family moves to Englewood, New Jersey, where Ward enters Englewood High School as a freshman. Father becomes deeply involved in the work of the National Civil Liberties Bureau, an organization dedicated to protecting all Americans' right to free speech.

1919   Ward joins staff of the Englewood *Oracle*, the school newspaper and yearbook, for which he will be art editor and a contributor of drawings and cartoons through the end of his sophomore year. "At some point during my teen-age years," he will write in 1974, "I saw a linoleum block made and printed. . . . I remember shortly thereafter using gouges on a linoleum block of my own."

1920   In January, the American Civil Liberties Union (ACLU) is founded, and Harry F. Ward is elected chairman of the board, a position he will hold for twenty years.

1922   Ward graduates from Englewood High School with honors in art, mathematics, and debate; as part of Class Day ceremonies he interprets a favorite speech, Edmund Burke's "On Conciliation with the Colonies." In fall enrolls at Teachers College, Columbia University, to study fine arts; four-year curriculum focuses on theory of design, art history, and methods in art education but also includes courses in drawing, painting, sculpture, and printmaking. Ward's mentors among the Columbia studio faculty include John P. Heins, drawing and lithography, and Albert C. Heckman, etching and block printing. Joins the staff of the *Jester*, the Columbia humor magazine, to which he contributes drawings and cartoons throughout his undergraduate years.

1923   In the fall, on a blind date arranged by his roommate, meets May Yonge McNeer (b. Tampa, Fla., 1902), a newly admitted sophomore at the Columbia School of Journalism. A fellow-Methodist with a passion for Dickens, Mark Twain, and children's literature, May spent her freshman year as the first female undergraduate at the University of Georgia after a stint as the women's page editor of the Tampa *Morning Tribune*; she is as self-possessed and outgoing as Ward is shy and socially diffident. The couple's courtship, at first uncertain, deepens into a romance over the next three years.

1925   Serves as editor-in-chief of the Columbia *Jester*, and contributes two or three illustrated how-to articles on arts and crafts to Methodist youth publications.

1926   Ward and May McNeer graduate from Columbia University; days later, on June 11, they marry in a private ceremony at Union Theological Seminary, Harry F. Ward presiding. From mid-June through mid-September, the couple honeymoons in Scotland, England, and France before settling in Leipzig, where Ward is a special one-year student in printmaking at the Staatliche Akademie für graphische Kunst und Buchgewerbe (National Academy of Graphic Arts and Bookmaking). His teachers are Alois Kolb, etching; Georg Alexander Mathey, lithography; and Hans Alexander "Theodore" Mueller, wood engraving. Ward's admiration for Mueller, his work, and his example is profound and abiding. In his workshop at the Academy, Ward will later recall, Mueller "pursued his own projects, making prints, designing book jackets, illustrating," and in the classroom operated "less as a teacher than as a creative artist . . . always asking the question 'What is this material capable of that I haven't got out of it yet?' and always being able to spend the time necessary to find out. For me to be helped and guided by a man who was himself doing, and not just talking about it, was of tremendous importance."

1927   In a Leipzig bookstall, chances upon a copy of *Die Sonne* ("The Sun," 1919), a contemporary retelling of the myth of Icarus by the Belgian graphic artist Frans Masereel. This "wordless novel"—an album of sixty-three wood engravings that, when read in sequence, tell a complex story in purely visual terms— exerts a shaping influence on Ward's artistic ambitions. In fall returns to New York, where he meets a handful of editor-publishers especially enthusiastic about his portfolio: Louise Seaman, director of Macmillan's juvenile division; John Farrar and Margaret Petherbridge, of the newly founded Farrar & Rinehart; George Macy, the proprietor of Macy-Masius, a private press specializing in illustrated limited editions; and Harrison "Hal" Smith, editor-in-chief of Harcourt, Brace & Co.

1928   Ward's first book commission—eight brush drawings for *The Begging Deer: Stories of Japanese Children*, by Dorothy Rowe— published by Macmillan. (His drawings for Rowe's companion volume, *Travelling Shops: Stories of Chinese Children*, will be published the following year.) While helping Ward research the background for these illustrations, May McNeer undertakes her own retelling of Japanese folk tales; the result is *Prince Bantam*, with brush drawings by Ward (Macmillan, 1929). George Macy accepts Ward's proposal to illustrate Oscar Wilde's *Ballad of Reading Gaol* with twenty-five mezzotints. Harrison Smith commissions crayon drawings for *Little Blacknose*, a children's story by Hildegarde Hoyt Swift (Harcourt, Brace, 1929), who will become a favorite of Ward among his collaborators.

1929   Ward reads *Schicksal* ("Destiny," 1926), by the German engraver Otto Nückel, a wordless novel of great narrative complexity that challenges him to begin work on a wordless book of his own. By the end of March he has cut the first thirty blocks of *Gods' Man: A Novel in Woodcuts*; he shows the work-in-progress to Harrison Smith, who had recently left Harcourt to start his own firm in partnership with the London publisher Jonathan Cape. Smith immediately offers a contract, telling Ward that if the work were completed by the end of the summer, *Gods' Man* would be the lead title in Cape & Smith's first catalog. Working late every night in his and May's apartment-studio in Palisade, New Jersey, Ward cuts 110 more blocks in five months, and prints them on his newly purchased Washington flat-bed press. *Gods' Man* is published, in both trade and deluxe editions, in October. Despite being issued during the week of the Crash, it will sell more than twenty thousand copies over the next four years.

1930   In the February issue of *The Horn Book*, Ward publishes "Contemporary Book Illustration," a statement of first principles for book illustrators and their editors that criticizes the many artists who routinely execute "a set of pictures to be scattered through the pages of a book a few minutes before binding" and praises the few (Boris Artsybasheff, James Daugherty, Elizabeth MacKistry, and himself) who can conceive of a book as "a single unit from binding design to tailpiece." Collaborates with May on *Stop, Tim! The Tale of a Car* (Farrar & Rinehart), a picture book in two-color lithographs, and *Waif Maid* (Macmillan), a children's novel with six full-page multicolor woodcuts and fifteen pen-and-ink chapter headings. Harrison Smith commissions six wood engravings for the Alice Raphael translation of Goethe's *Faust*, published in both trade and deluxe editions. Farrar & Rinehart commissions sets of wood engravings for *Midsummernight* (1930), a novel by Carl Wilhelmson, and three new books by Alec Waugh: *Hot Countries* (1930), *Most Women* (1931), and *Thirteen Such Years* (1932). For Macmillan, Ward makes twelve watercolor illustrations for Elizabeth Coatesworth's *The*

Cat Who Went to Heaven (Newbery Award, 1931) and thirty multicolor woodcuts for May's abridged edition of Captain Marryat's *Children of the New Forest*. In October, second "novel in woodcuts," *Madman's Drum*, published in both trade and deluxe editions by Cape & Smith. On September 16, son, David Weedon Ward, born prematurely in Englewood Hospital; he lives only five days. The Wards spend the winter in Paris, where Lynd buys an accordion, the mastering of which, at first only a solace, becomes a lifelong pleasure.

1931   Ward now established and much in demand as a freelance designer of dust jackets, frontispieces, decorations, and illustrations for books for children, adults, and collectors. His working hours, according to May, are "from nine in the morning to midnight, seven days a week," a pace he will maintain well into his sixties. Wishing to create new opportunities for himself and other like-minded writers and illustrators, explores the possibility of organizing a non-commercial publishing house run on the cooperative model and dedicated to "the production of books in a more careful and hand-controlled manner than is possible in the ordinary publishing business." The Equinox Cooperative Press is incorporated in December. Its nine members include Ward and May; Ward's former teachers John Heins and Albert Heckman; Evelyn Harter, the production editor at Cape & Smith; and the fine-arts printer Lewis F. White. Equinox's "office" is White's printing shop (35 West 21st Street) but only after hours, on weeknights and on weekends; its "warehouse" is the boxroom of the Wards' New Jersey apartment.

1932   Equinox issues its first book (Llewelyn Powys's philosophical essay *Now That the Gods Are Dead*, with four wood engravings by Ward) and four hand-sewn poetry chapbooks (the "Equinox Quarters," including *This Earth* by William Faulkner and *A Christmas Poem* by Thomas Mann). Ward creates thirty full-page drawings for a two-volume edition of Charles Reade's *The Cloister and the Hearth*, published by George Macy's new venture, the Limited Editions Club. In November, his third "novel in woodcuts," *Wild Pilgrimage*, published by Harrison Smith and his new business partner, Robert Haas. Daughter, Nanda Weedon Ward, born August 5.

Chronology

1933   Father, though not a member of the Communist Party, becomes chairman of the American League Against War and Fascism, a "Popular Front" organization funded by the Party, promoted by ecumenical clergy, and dedicated to resisting the rise of fascism in Europe. Equinox issues *We Need One Another*, an essay on the sexes by D. H. Lawrence; *Three Blue Suits*, short stories by Aline Bernstein; and *Prelude to a Million Years*, a short narrative in wood engravings by Ward. For Smith & Haas, Ward provides four wood engravings for *A Green Bough*, poems by William Faulkner, and four lithographs for *Southern Mail*, a novel by Antoine de Saint-Exupéry. For his father, creates four lithographs for the polemical essay *In Place of Profit: Social Incentives in the Soviet Union* (Scribners).

1934   Ward joins the Artists' Union, an organization dedicated to improving economic opportunities for New York City artists and to shaping the agenda of the Public Works of Art Project, precursor to the WPA's Federal Arts Project. Illustrates Mary Shelley's *Frankenstein* with fifteen full-page wood engravings, fifteen chapter headings, and several decorative vignettes; it is published in a deluxe, slipcased edition by Smith & Haas. Equinox issues *Nocturnes*, three stories by Thomas Mann with seven lithographs by Ward.

1935   Provides decorations for *An Almanac for Moderns*, a daybook by the Chicago-based naturalist, historian, and essayist Donald Culross Peattie (Putnam); Ward will also decorate Peattie's *Book of Hours* (Putnam, 1937), *Journey into America* (Houghton Mifflin, 1943), and *A Cup of Sky* (Houghton Mifflin, 1950). With Stuart Davis, Max Weber, and other artists "conscious of the need of collective action against war and fascism," becomes a founding member of the American Artists' Congress (AAC), an organization modeled on the American Writers' Congress and closely allied to the Artists' Union. Equinox issues *One of Us*, a young-adult biography of John Reed told in thirty lithographs by Ward and a brief text by Granville Hicks.

1936   On February 15–17, the AAC, with some 360 active members, convenes in New York City; Ward, one of thirty-four artist-speakers, delivers a talk at the New School for Social Research on race, nationality, and art in Nazi Germany and the United

States. With Alex R. Stavenitz, chairman of the graphic-arts committee of the AAC, plans an exhibition of contemporary American prints scheduled to open simultaneously in dozens of U.S. cities "to help the print reach a public comparable in size to that of the book and the motion picture." *Song Without Words*, a "prose poem" in wood engravings, printed in a limited edition by Random House (now incorporating Smith & Haas). *PM*, a trade magazine for production managers and art directors, publishes a special Lynd Ward number, which includes two essays by Ward: an appreciation of Masereel, Mueller, and other "woodcutters of our time," and a piece on how to cut a woodblock. On December 2, "America Today: 100 Prints Chosen and Exhibited by the American Artists' Congress" opens in thirty venues from coast to coast. Ward is one of the show's ten jurors and, via Equinox, the publisher of the exhibition catalogue.

1937   In February Ward named supervisor of the Graphic Arts Division of the New York Chapter of the Federal Arts Project; he and the seventy artists reporting to him produce five thousand prints a year, which are distributed by the state to hospitals, schools, and other public institutions. Gives lessons in wood engraving at the American Artists' School, the successor institution to the John Reed Club School of Art. Begins work on his most ambitious illustration project, the Limited Editions Club's five-volume set of Victor Hugo's *Les Misérables* (1938), for which he provides more than five hundred line drawings (five frontispieces, three hundred chapter headings, and two hundred decorative spots). *Vertigo*, Ward's final "novel in woodcuts," published in November by Random House. Second daughter, Robin Kendall Ward, born November 25.

1938   On the eve of World War II, Ward helps Hans Alexander Mueller and his Jewish wife leave Germany and relocate to Scarsdale, New York. Finds Mueller an adjunct teaching position on the Columbia faculty, writes an article on his work for *PM* magazine, and gives him a $100 advance against royalties on *Woodcuts and Wood Engravings*, a how-to book for Equinox. When the book, which requires five-color printing, becomes too costly for Equinox to publish, Ward sells the press's rights in the work to the fine-arts publisher Pynson Printers for $500. With the press in the black, Mueller's book in capable hands, and no future projects under contract, the members of Equinox, having published sixteen titles over seven years, vote to dissolve their cooperative, effective December 9.

1939   The New York-based Artists' Union enlarges its scope to become the national Union of American Artists (UAA), an affiliate of the CIO; Ward resigns from the Federal Arts Project to become the UAA's first chairman. In September, father's American League Against War and Fascism collapses in the wake of the German-Soviet non-aggression pact.

1940   Begins a seventh wordless book, "Hymn for the Night," a retelling of the Mary and Joseph story set in Nazi Germany; cuts twenty-odd blocks and then shelves the project, partly due to the press of time, "partly because the subject . . . was once removed from experience rather than being immediately my own." Ward abandons the "woodcut novel" as a form, reserving wood engraving almost exclusively for independent prints—"individual works that exist entirely for their own sake"—which he makes on his Washington flat-bed press in unlimited editions, filling individual and gallery orders upon request. ("I want people who like the prints to be able to have them and to afford them," he will later say. "Perhaps it's just my Methodist background emerging, but to artificially produce scarcity is *wrong*.") He begins to experiment more freely in other media, illustrating *Beowulf* with sixteen full-page color lithographs (Heritage Press, 1940) and decorating *The Count of Monte Cristo* with two hundred brush drawings (Limited Editions Club, 1941). Hires an agent, Nettie King, who will negotiate contracts, solicit commissions, and be a close friend for the rest of his working life. At the suggestion of the fine-arts faculty at Teachers College, creates forty-two captionless drawings conforming to the specifications of Columbia psychologist Percival M. Symonds and designed to elicit fantasy narratives from adolescent subjects. These pictures, the basis of the so-called Symonds Picture-Story Test, are widely used by psychoanalysts throughout the 1940s and 1950s. (Clinical results of the test, and the drawings themselves, are published in Symonds's book *Adolescent Fantasy: An Investigation of the*

Picture-Story Method of Personality Study, Columbia University Press, 1949.)

1941 Father, at age sixty-eight, retires from both the Union Theological Seminary and the ACLU, but pledges four more years to the MFSS. In January, the membership of the AAC is split over the Soviet invasion of Eastern Europe, with the majority, led by Ward, supporting or expressing neutrality toward the Soviets, and the "dissidents"—led by Meyer Schapiro and including AAC founders Stuart Davis and Max Weber—forming the rival, anti-Stalinist Federation of Modern Painters and Sculptors.

1942 Presented the annual prize of the Carteret Book Club, a New Jersey society of fine printers, book artists, and book collectors. Creates lithographs for a collector's edition of Hemingway's *For Whom the Bell Tolls* (Limited Editions Club), a hundred ink drawings for *Gargantua and Pantagruel* (Heritage Press), and dozens of brush drawings for Edgar Lee Masters's *The Sangamon* (Farrar & Rinehart), a study of life on the Sangamon and Spoon rivers of Illinois. With Hildegarde Hoyt Swift, creates the enduring picture book *The Little Red Lighthouse and the Great Gray Bridge* (Harcourt, Brace). In April, the decimated AAC merges with the UAA to form the Artists' League of America, with Rockwell Kent as its first president; Ward refuses a leadership role but remains an active member until the League disbands in 1950.

1943 Illustrates Esther Forbes's bestselling *Johnny Tremain* (Newbery Award, 1944), a tale of Boston during the American Revolution, which inaugurates Ward's long relationship with Houghton Mifflin and children's editor Mary Silva Cosgrave. Creates ten full-page mezzotints for Erasmus's *In Praise of Folly* (Limited Editions Club). In the fall, Ward, age thirty-eight and the father of two, is enlisted into the wartime labor force; accepts a two-year assignment assembling gyroscopes at Bendix Aviation, Teterboro, New Jersey. For convenience' sake, family moves from Palisade to Leonia, New Jersey, where Ward converts a barn on the property into an art studio.

1944 Ward makes color lithographs for a collector's edition of Richard Hughes's novel *The Innocent Voyage* (*A High Wind in Jamaica*), published by Heritage Press. Does color-crayon drawings for *The Gold Rush* (Grosset & Dunlap), a small-format picture book by May McNeer commissioned by the Artists & Writer Guild, packagers of the Little Golden Books.

1945   Elected an Associate Member in Graphic Arts of the National Academy of Design, New York City.

1946   Makes color drawings for Esther Forbes's young-adult biography *America's Paul Revere*, his first of many contributions to Houghton Mifflin's "America's" series and a Caldecott Honor Book for 1947. Provides brush drawings and color plates for an abridged edition of *Robinson Crusoe* in Grosset & Dunlap's Illustrated Junior Library; he will later provide illustrations for *Kidnapped* (1948) and an abridged *Swiss Family Robinson* (1949) in the same series.

1947   Makes lithographs for May's book *The Golden Flash* (Viking Press), the story of a fire engine in Old New York, and Hildegard Hoyt Swift's *North Star Shining: A Pictorial History of the American Negro* (Morrow). In fall awarded the Zella de Milhau Prize of the American Institute of Graphic Arts for "Bridges at Echo Bay," a six-by-nine-inch wood engraving cut that summer at Lonely Lake. Ward is successfully sponsored for membership in the Society of American Etchers, Gravers, Lithographers, and Woodcutters (SAEGLW) by the society's president, etcher John Taylor Arms.

1948   "Clouded Over," a six-by-nine-inch wood engraving depicting children at play in a woodland landscape, wins the Joseph Pennell Purchase Prize at the sixth annual American Print Exhibition at the Library of Congress. Over the next four years, Ward does an occasional series of portraits, mostly in oils, for the cover of *The Atlantic Monthly*; subjects include Somerset Maugham, General William Donovan, and Evelyn Waugh, but he refuses the magazine's request for a portrait of J. Edgar Hoover.

1949   In spring "Seedling," an eight-by-six-inch wood engraving of a planter restoring life to a ruined forest, wins the National Academy of Design's award for the year's best print. Ward illustrates

Chronology

Stewart Holbrook's full-color picture book *America's Ethan Allen* (Houghton Mifflin), a Caldecott Honor Book for 1950.

1950   May writes a young-adult history, *The California Gold Rush*, for Random House's Landmark Books series, to which Ward contributes sixty brush drawings; in 1960 the Wards will do *The Alaska Gold Rush* in the same series.

1951   Ward illustrates Henry Steele Commager's full-color picture book *America's Robert E. Lee* (Houghton Mifflin). May publishes *John Wesley* (Abington Press), a young-adult biography of the founder of Methodism, with color and black-and-white lithographs by Ward; in 1953 the Wards will collaborate on a companion volume, *Martin Luther.*

1952   Makes dozens of small color lithographs for Tennyson's *Idylls of the King* (Limited Editions Club). Provides brush drawings for Jeannette C. Nolan's *The Story of Robert E. Lee* (Grosset & Dunlap) and for May's young-adult novel *Up a Crooked River* (Viking Press), a family adventure set in the Florida swamps of 1871. With his older daughter, the writer Nanda Ward, creates a black-crayon picture book, *The Black Sombrero* (Ariel Books); they will later collaborate on two more picture books, *The High-Flying Hat* (Ariel, 1956) and *Hi Tom* (Hastings House, 1962). Writes and illustrates his first picture book for children, *The Biggest Bear* (Houghton Mifflin), the story of a farm boy who adopts a bear cub and must decide what to do when it grows too big to keep. The forty full-page casein paintings, full of details pulled from his Lonely Lake sketchbooks, are done in black, white, and sepia.

1953   On June 23 in Los Angeles, receives the 1953 Caldecott Medal for picture book of the year, awarded by the American Library Association to *The Biggest Bear.* Ward's acceptance speech, and a memoir by May, appear in the August issue of *The Horn Book,* and Houghton Mifflin has a copy of the book specially bound in black bearskin as a congratulatory keepsake. Ward elected president of SAGA: The Society of American Graphic Artists (formerly SAEGLW); during his six-year term he will refine the society's mission "to promote printmaking as a fine art, honor artists of integrity and skill, and exhibit work in a diversity of styles and printmaking processes and techniques." May publishes the nonfiction picture book *The Mexican Story* (Ariel Books), with sixty-five color and black-and-white brush drawings by Ward; the Wards will also do *The Canadian Story* (1958) and *The American Indian Story* (1963) in the same series. In July, during the House Un-American Activities hearings, Manning R. Johnson, once a senior member of the American Communist Party, names Harry F. Ward, former chairman of the American League Against War and Fascism, "the chief architect for Communist infiltration and subversion in the religious field." Although he is never called before HUAC, father now finds himself blacklisted by editors of most mainstream publications and his movements scrutinized by the FBI.

1954   George Macy presents Ward with the Silver Medal of the Limited Editions Club, awarded for twenty-five years of excellence in book illustration. Ward illustrates *War Chief of the Seminoles* (Random House), a Landmark Book about Osceola, and *Little Baptiste* (Houghton Mifflin), a picture book set in the French Canadian woods, both written by May.

1957   Ward makes eighty-five brush drawings for the Heritage Press collector's edition of Dickens's *Our Mutual Friend*. Illustrates May's full-color picture book *America's Abraham Lincoln* (Houghton Mifflin) and her collection of inspirational brief lives, *Armed with Courage* (Abington Press). Decorates Hildegarde Hoyt Swift's *The Edge of April* (Morrow), a biography of the American naturalist and writer John Burroughs. Sister, Muriel, dies suddenly of an aortic aneurism, August 11; mother begins steep decline into dementia and, ultimately, confinement in a New Jersey nursing home.

1958   Both of their daughters having left home, the Wards move from Leonia to a small house in nearby Cresskill, New Jersey. They add a studio that doubles the house's size, and Ward, improving the property, indulges his hobby of designing and doing stonework—fireplaces, walkways, and retaining walls—as a respite from book illustration. Creates a new set of brush drawings and black-and-sepia casein paintings for the twenty-fifth-anniversary edition of Elizabeth Coatesworth's *The Cat Who Went to Heaven* (Simon & Schuster). Named an

Academician in Graphic Arts by the National Academy of Design.

1959   Makes twenty color lithographs for Joseph Conrad's *Lord Jim* (Limited Editions Club).

1960   The Wards publish *My Friend Mac* (Houghton Mifflin), a sequel to *Little Baptiste* (1954). Mother dies, November 20, at age eighty-seven.

1961   Makes eighteen two-color lithographs and eighteen brush drawings for Thomas Paine's *The Rights of Man* (Limited Editions Club).

1962   Ward collaborates with May on the full-color picture book *America's Mark Twain* (Houghton Mifflin). Decorates Hildegarde Hoyt Swift's *From the Eagle's Wings* (Morrow), a biography of the American environmentalist John Muir, and provides thirty-seven brush drawings for Katharine Miller's *Five Plays by Shakespeare* (Houghton Mifflin). Awarded the John Taylor Arms Memorial Prize of the National Academy of Design for the sixteen-by-six-inch wood engraving "Two Men." Accepts perhaps his most ambitious commission: three oil-painting murals for the planned national offices of the United Methodist Church in Evanston, Illinois, a project he will develop and execute over the next seven years.

1963   On October 15, the ninetieth birthday of Harry F. Ward celebrated with an evening of tributes at Carnegie Hall, concluding with a speech by the guest of honor protesting the nuclear arms race, U.S. foreign policy in Viet Nam, and the government's undermining of the Bill of Rights in the name of national security. For the cover of a privately printed booklet commemorating the event, Ward cuts an iconic portrait-block of his father.

1964   Illustrates May's *Give Me Freedom* (Abington Press), a sequel to *Armed with Courage* (1957).

1965   Ward's second picture book, *Nic of the Woods*, the story of a city dog who accompanies his master on a summer in the Canadian wild, published by Houghton Mifflin. Makes twenty-eight two-color lithographs for Robert Louis Stevenson's *The Master of Ballantrae* (Limited Editions Club).

1966   Receives the Samuel F. B. Morse Gold Medal, the highest award given by the National Academy of Design, for the seven-by-thirteen-inch wood engraving "Flower Girl." World Publishing of Cleveland, Ohio, reprints *Gods' Man* and, the following year, *Wild Pilgrimage* in inexpensive hardcover editions, and Ward's images become part of the visual vocabulary of the emerging sixties' counterculture. Father dies December 9, at age ninety-three. His memorial service, held the following January 4th at James Memorial Chapel, Union Theological Seminary, is attended by four hundred friends, colleagues, and admirers.

1967   Provides fifty-two lithograph decorations for *The Writings of Thomas Jefferson* (Limited Editions Club). Illustrates May's *The Wolf of Lamb's Lane* (Houghton Mifflin), a contemporary retelling of Little Red Riding Hood set in suburban Cresskill, New Jersey, and *Go Tim Go!* (L. W. Singer Co.), a second edition of their first picture book, *Stop, Tim!* (1930).

1969   On May 18, the national office of the United Methodist Church opens with the public display of Ward's three murals, one depicting the life of John Wesley, the others symbolic of the growth of Methodism in America and of the church's ministry throughout the world. Ward receives the Rutgers University Library Award for his lifetime contribution to children's literature.

1971   For Houghton Mifflin, illustrates two historical novels for young readers: May's *Stranger in the Pines* (1971), set in the New Jersey Pine Barrens of the 1880s, and Scott O'Dell's *The Treasure of Topo-el-Bampo* (1972), set in the Mexico of the mid-1700s.

1973   Ward's third and final picture book, the wordless story *The Silver Pony*, published by Houghton Mifflin. The tale of a lonely, daydreaming farm boy who escapes into fantasy on an imagined flying horse, this book—a set of eighty black-and-white paintings that, like the images in the "novels in woodcuts," are reproduced only on the recto pages—is a Caldecott Honor Book and a Boston Globe–Horn Book book of the year. At the invitation of publisher Harry N. Abrams, Ward begins planning a self-selected monograph honoring his lifework in wood engraving.

1974   In May, *Storyteller Without Words: The Wood Engravings of Lynd Ward* published by Abrams. This large-format book—11" x 11", 384 pages, with 710 reproductions and a text by Ward—collects all six wordless novels; selected illustrations for *Frankenstein*, *Faust*, and other early books; thirty-nine independent prints, 1933–71; and examples of his bookplates, spot illustrations, and other minor work. "Because it is all of the books and most of the blocks," Ward writes in his dedication, "this book is for May." A solo exhibition of forty-six independent prints, "Lynd Ward: Wood Engravings 1929–1974," is on view May 13–31 at Associated American Artists, New York, Ward's chief print dealer since 1934.

1975   Ward suggests that the Limited Editions Club, in celebration of the bicentennial of the United States, commission an edition of Edmund Burke's writings on the American Revolution; the result—*On Conciliation with the Colonies and Other Papers*, edited by Peter J. Stanlis—is illustrated with twenty-five duotone wood engravings by Ward. In September, Ward and May McNeer jointly receive the Regina Medal of the Catholic Library Association for their "continued distinguished contribution to children's literature."

1976   May publishes *Bloomsday for Maggie* (Houghton Mifflin), an autobiographical fiction about an eighteen-year-old "girl reporter" in Prohibition-era Florida, with drawings by Ward. Heartened by the reception of *The Silver Pony* and *Storyteller Without Words*, Ward begins making sketches for a new wordless "novel in woodcuts." *Bibliognost*, a little magazine for book collectors, publishes a *Festschrift* for Ward at age seventy, featuring an interview with Ward by editor Gil Williams and memoirs by May McNeer, Evelyn Harter, Mary Silva Cosgrave, and others.

Chronology

1977   Ward completes two final projects, both commissioned by
         the Boston publisher and printmaker Michael McCurdy: six
         wood engravings for Anthony Hecht's translation of Voltaire's
         Poem Upon the Lisbon Disaster (1977), and the headpiece for a
         broadside of "Moloch," a section of *Howl*, by Allen Ginsberg
         (1978). In July, during what is perhaps his sixtieth summer at
         Lonely Lake, suffers a bleeding ulcer and loses nearly six pints
         of blood. He is hospitalized in Sault Ste. Marie but never fully
         recovers his health, and soon experiences depression, chronic
         fatigue, and short-term memory loss.

1978   Draws a new frontispiece portrait of Thomas Paine for the
         Easton Press reprint of his 1961 *Rights of Man*. Diagnosed
         with Alzheimer's disease. Ceases to take new commissions, but
         continues to design and cut blocks for his novel-in-progress,
         never to be completed.

1979   In spring, May persuades Ward that they should leave New
         Jersey to be near their daughters, Nanda and Robin, both of
         whom live with their families in suburban Washington, D.C.
         Ward donates his Washington flat-bed press to the art depart-
         ment of Dwight Morrow High School, the successor institu-
         tion to Englewood High, and, after a summer at Lonely Lake,
         moves with May to Reston, Virginia, and into permanent re-
         tirement.

1985   Dies at home, June 28, two days after his eightieth birthday. His
         body is cremated, and his ashes kept by the family. As was May's
         wish, upon her death, in July 1994, her ashes are commingled
         with his and, the following summer, are scattered by Nanda
         and Robin on the waters of Lonely Lake.

NOTE ON THE TEXTS

This volume contains three books by Lynd Ward—*Prelude to a Million Years* (1933), *Song Without Words* (1936), and *Vertigo* (1937)—as well as texts of five essays written by Ward in the mid-1970s.

Prelude to a Million Years was published in the fall of 1933 by Equinox Cooperative Press, New York, in an edition limited to 920 numbered copies signed by the artist. The boxwood printing blocks were engraved by Ward in 1932–33. They were printed by Lewis F. White, New York, who also designed the typography. The printed sheets were sewn, and the books hand-bound, by associates of Equinox Cooperative Press. Ward's binding-board design, stenciled on black paper with airbrushed gold ink, has been adapted for the endpapers of the present volume. The spine, a copper foil strip embossed with the book's title, was sewn to the boards with black string. The woodblocks for the book are in the collection of the Prints and Photographs Division, Library of Congress, Washington, D.C.

The images constituting *Prelude to a Million Years* in the present volume are reproduced from a copy of the Equinox edition. They have not been resized: the dimensions are those of the original prints. The typographic half-title page and the typographic copyright page have been deleted.

Song Without Words was published in the fall of 1936 by Random House, New York, in an edition of 1,250 numbered copies signed by the artist. The blocks were engraved by Ward in 1935. They were printed by Lewis F. White, New York, who also designed the typography. The words "SONG WITHOUT WORDS" on the title page were printed in scarlet. The book was bound by the H. Wolff Book Manufacturing Co., New York. The binding was metallic copper paper over boards with a white cloth spine, and the book was sold in a metallic copper slipcase. The woodblocks for the book are in the Lynd Ward Collection, Joseph M. Lauinger Memorial Library, Georgetown University, Washington, D.C.

The images constituting *Song Without Words* in the present volume are reproduced from a copy of the Random House edition. They have not been resized; the dimensions are those of the original prints. The typographic half-title page and the typographic copyright page have been deleted.

Vertigo was published in November 1937 by Random House, New York. The blocks were engraved by Ward in 1935–37 and were then made into electrotypes—that is, they were reproduced as metal printing plates in molds made from the original woodblocks. The electrotypes were made by Flower Electrotypes, New York City. The typography was by Lewis F. White, who also designed the typographic dust jacket. The book was printed by the Plimpton Press, Norwood, Massachusetts. The engraved word "VERTIGO" on the title page was printed in Wedgwood blue. The book was bound by the H. Wolff Book Manufacturing Co., New York, in tan cloth on which an image by Ward—a downward spiral against a nightscape studded with stars—was printed in black ink. Of the 234 woodblocks for the book, 232 are in the John DePol Collection of American Wood Engravings, Department of Rare Books and Special Collections, Rutgers University Library, New Brunswick, New Jersey. The whereabouts of the other two blocks are unknown.

The images constituting *Vertigo* in the present volume are reproduced from a copy of the Random House edition. They have not been resized; the dimensions are those of the original prints. The typographic half-title page and the typographic copyright page have been deleted.

Four of the five prose works collected under the heading "Essays" were written by Ward for *Storyteller Without Words: The Wood Engravings of Lynd Ward* (New York: Harry N. Abrams, 1974). In that volume, the essays "On 'Prelude to a Million Years,' " "On 'Song Without Words,' " and "On 'Vertigo,' " appeared as untitled prefaces to the three books reprinted here, and "The Book and the Woodblock" appeared as an untitled preface to a selection of Ward's book illustrations. The remaining essay, "The Equinox Idea," first appeared as the untitled foreword to *A Relevant Memoir: The Story of the Equinox Cooperative Press*, by Henry Hart (New York: Three Mountains Press, 1977). The present volume reprints the texts of the essays found in *Storyteller Without Words* and *A Relevant Memoir*, but under titles supplied by the publisher with the consent of the author's estate.

NOTES

In the notes below, the reference numbers denote page and line of this volume (the line count includes headings). No note is made for material included in standard desk-reference books such as Webster's *Collegiate*, *Biographical*, and *Geographical* dictionaries. For further biographical background than is contained in the Chronology, see *Storyteller Without Words: The Wood Engravings of Lynd Ward* (New York: Harry N. Abrams, 1974), *A Relevant Memoir: The Story of the Equinox Cooperative Press*, by Henry Hart (New York: Three Mountains Press, 1977), *Labor-Religion Prophet: The Times and Life of Harry F. Ward*, by Eugene P. Link (Boulder, Colo.: Westview Press, 1984), and *In the Trenches with Jesus and Marx: Harry F. Ward and the Struggle for Social Justice*, by David Nelson Duke (Tuscaloosa: University of Alabama Press, 2003); see also "Lynd Ward," by May McNeer, *The Horn Book*, 29:4 (August 1953), and the special Lynd Ward numbers of *PM: An Intimate Journal for Production Managers, Art Directors, and Their Associates* (2:6, February 1936) and *Bibliognost: The Book Collector's Little Magazine* (2:2, May 1976). For critical studies of Lynd Ward's novels in woodcuts, see *Wordless Books: The Original Graphic Novels*, by David A. Beronä (New York: Harry N. Abrams, 2008), and Mr. Beronä's introductions to the Dover reprint editions of *Madman's Drum* (2005), *Vertigo* (2008), and *"Prelude to a Million Years" and "Song Without Words": Two Graphic Novels* (2010); see also "The Novel in Woodcuts: A Handbook," by Martin S. Cohen, *Journal of*

Modern Literature, 6:2 (April 1977), *The Silent Shout: Frans Masereel, Lynd Ward, and the Novel in Woodcuts*, by Perry Willett (Bloomington: Indiana University Libraries, 1997), and *Vertigo: A Graphic Novel of the Great Depression*, by Michael Joseph (New Brunswick, N.J.: Rutgers University Libraries, 2003). A volume of special interest is *Lynd Ward's Last, Unfinished Wordless Novel*, with an introduction by Michael McCurdy (New Brunswick, N.J.: Rutgers University Libraries/New Jersey Book Arts Symposium, 2001). This small book, privately printed in an edition of 125 copies, documents a work that Ward began at age seventy but soon became too ill to complete; it prints, directly from the original blocks, twenty-six images from a planned series of forty-four, with a prose description of the unfinished blocks by Michael Joseph.

The editor and the publisher wish to thank Robert Dance, author of the unpublished manuscript "Lynd Ward, Book Artist: Biography + Bibliography," and Robert Young Jr., author of the unpublished essay "Lynd Ward: An Appreciation and an Account," for their contributions to the Chronology. Special thanks to Robin Ward Savage and Nanda Weedon Ward for their generosity, their editorial counsel, and their trust.

ON "PRELUDE TO A MILLION YEARS"

641.6 a well-known painter] Thomas Hart Benton (1889–1975), Missouri-born American Regionalist whose paintings, murals, and lithographs depicted the plight of the rural Midwest during the Depression years. From 1912 to 1935 he lived in Greenwich Village—in poverty, squalor, and antagonism with the New York art world. Benton's fortunes changed in 1934, when his dealer, Maynard Walker, a friend of Henry Luce, arranged a cover article on him and his work in *Time* Magazine, which led not only to increased gallery sales but to his returning to Missouri as a well-paid instructor at the Kansas City Art Institute.

641.14 "Artists' Life"] *Künstlerleben*, op. 316 (1867), by Johann Strauss II.

644.5–6 a beautiful rag paper] Canson & Montgolfier's Vidalon Velin.

644.7 a group of young people] The Equinox Cooperative Press was incorporated in December 1931; its nine original members, each holding twenty shares at five dollars each, were Ward (president) and McNeer (secretary); Ward's former teachers John Heins (who designed the pressmark, right) and Albert Heckman, both of the fine-arts faculty at Teachers College, Columbia University; Lewis F. White, a book designer, photographer, and fine-arts printer; Evelyn Harter, managing editor at Cape & Smith, who named the firm "Equinox"; and three of Harter's friends in publishing: Henry Hart, an editor-publicist at Scribners; Belle Rosenbaum, assistant to Irita Van Doren at the *Herald Tribune*'s Sunday book review; and Mabel Remont, the press's business manager. Later members included Harter's husband, Milton B. "Tony" Glick, a designer for The Viking Press, who succeeded Lewis F. White; and financial experts Stanley K. Oldden and Mildred Myers, who in 1935 together succeeded Mabel Remont, arranged for professional distribution of books to the trade, and provided Equinox free office space at 444 Madison Avenue. In five and a half years, Equinox published sixteen titles, the first in spring 1932, the last in fall 1937.

THE EQUINOX IDEA

647.20–21 that handful of books] The following is a checklist of publications by the Equinox Cooperative Press:

> *Now That the Gods Are Dead*, a philosophical essay by Llewelyn Powys, with four wood engravings by Lynd Ward. Hardcover (no dust jacket), 52 pages, 1932. Limited to 400 numbered copies, signed by the author and illustrator.
> *This Earth*, a poem by William Faulkner, with drawings by Albert Heckman. The Equinox Quarters, No. 1. Hand-sewn in paper wraps, 8 pages, 1932.

A Visit from St. Nicholas, a poem by Clement C. Moore.
The Equinox Quarters, No. 2. Hand-sewn in paper
wraps, 8 pages, 1932.

A Christmas Poem, by Thomas Mann, translated from the
German by Henry Hart, with four wood engravings
by Lynd Ward. The Equinox Quarters, No. 3. Hand-
sewn in paper wraps, 8 pages, 1932.

Prelude, a poem by Conrad Aiken, with drawings by John
P. Heins. The Equinox Quarters, No. 4. Hand-sewn
in paper wraps, 8 pages, 1932.

We Need One Another, an essay by D. H. Lawrence, introduction by Henry Hart, with drawings by John P.
Heins. Hardcover (no dust jacket), 36 pages plus four
tipped-in illustrations, 1933.

Prelude to a Million Years, a book of wood engravings by
Lynd Ward. Hand-bound hardcover (no dust jacket),
72 pages, 1933. Limited to 920 numbered copies,
signed by the artist.

Three Blue Suits, short stories by Aline Bernstein ("Mr.
Froelich," "Herbert Wilson," "Eugene"), with a frontispiece by John P. Heins. Hardcover (in slipcase), 32
pages plus tipped-in frontispiece, 1933. Limited to
600 numbered copies, signed by the author.

Nocturnes, short stories by Thomas Mann ("A Gleam,"
"Railway Accident," "A Weary Hour"), translated
from the German by H. T. Lowe-Porter, with seven
lithographs by Lynd Ward. Hardcover (in slipcase),
64 pages, 1934. Limited to 1,000 numbered copies,
signed by the author.

Comrade: Mister, poems by Isidore Schneider, with two
pen drawings by Guyula Zilzer. Hardcover (in dust
jacket), 48 pages, 1934.

One of Us: The Story of John Reed, told in 30 lithographs
by Lynd Ward (on recto pages), with a narrative by

Granville Hicks (on verso pages). Hardcover (in dust
jacket), 64 pages plus tipped-in title page, 1935.*

Imperial Hearst: A Social Biography, by Ferdinand Lundberg,
with a preface by Dr. Charles A. Beard. Hardcover (in
dust jacket), 408 pages, 1935.

America Today: A Book of 100 *Prints Chosen and Exhibited
by the American Artists' Congress*, anonymously edited by Lynd Ward for the AAC, with introductory
essays by Alex R. Stavenitz ("The Origin of These
Prints"), Ralph M. Pearson ("These Prints and the
Public"), H. Glintenkamp ("The Woodcut"), Harry
Sternberg ("Etching"), and Louis Lozowick ("Lithography"). Catalogue of a nation-wide exhibition
of contemporary prints on view simultaneously in 30
American cities during December 1936. The prints,
reproduced in black-and-white on recto pages only,
include works by Paul Cadmus, Miguel Covarrubias,
Fritz Eichenberg, Philip Evergood, Wanda Gág, William Gropper, Rockwell Kent, J. J. Lankes, Raphael
Soyer, Lynd Ward (a wood engraving from *Wild Pilgrimage*), and Max Weber. Hardcover (in dust jacket),
216 pages, 1936.

Freud and Marx: A Dialectical Study, by Reuben Osborn,
with an introduction by John Strachey. Hardcover (in
dust jacket), 288 pages, 1937.

False Security: The Betrayal of the American Investor, by Ber-
nard J. Reis, with an introduction by John T. Flynn.
Hardcover (in dust jacket), 364 pages, 1937.

The Writer in a Changing World, edited by Henry Hart, with
an introduction by Joseph Freeman. The proceedings
of the Second American Writers' Congress, June 1937.
Essays by Newton Arvin, Carlton Beals, B. A. Botkin,
Karl Browder, Kenneth Burke, Malcolm Cowley,
Martha Gellhorn, Henry Hart, Ernest Hemingway,

Granville Hicks, Eugene Holmes, Archibald Macleish, Harry Slochower, Donald Ogden Stewart, Albert Rhys Williams, and Frances Winwar, followed by an unsigned account of the Congress by Henry Hart. Hardcover (in dust jacket), 256 pages, 1937.

THE BOOK AND THE WOODBLOCK

658.28–29 Michael Wohlgemut . . . Dürer] Among the book illustrations of Michael Wohlgemut (1434–1519) are the 1,809 woodcuts for the *Historia Mundi* (or *Nuremberg Chronicle*) of Hartmann Schedel (Nuremberg, 1493); of Lucas Cranach the Elder (1472–1553), the 100 woodcuts for Martin Luther's German rendering of the New Testament (Wittenberg, 1522); and of Albrecht Dürer (1471–1528), the woodcuts for *Four Books on Measurement*, a treatise on linear geometry (Nuremberg, 1525), and the *Four Books on Human Proportion*, a study in human anatomy (Nuremberg, 1527).

659.22 Thomas Bewick] Bewick, like John James Audubon, was a naturalist as well as an artist; his most important books are *A General History of the Quadrupeds* (1790) and the two-volume *History of British Birds* (*Land Birds*, 1797; *Water Birds*, 1804). He also illustrated Aesop's fables (1818) and volumes of poems by Oliver Goldsmith and Thomas Parnell. His *Memoir of Thomas Bewick, by Himself*, was published in 1862.

660.19 Gustave Doré] Doré's first major commission was the *Droll Tales* of Balzac (1855), for which he provided 425 engravings; other significant works include illustrations for Dante's *Divine Comedy* (*Inferno*, 1857; *Purgatorio* and *Paradiso*, 1867), Perrault's fairy tales (1862), Cervantes' *Don Quixote* (1863, see below), a folio Bible in English (1866), La Fontaine's fables (1867), Coleridge's *Rime of the Ancient Mariner* (1870), Blanchard Jarrold's journalistic *London: A Pilgrimage* (1872), and Poe's *The Raven* (1884).

660.27 *Don Quixote*] Doré produced 370 illustrations for the first complete French translation of Cervantes' comic masterpiece, published in two folio volumes by Hachette, Paris, in 1863.

661.22 *Frankenstein*] Ward himself did a set of wood engravings for Mary Shelley's novel (New York: Smith & Haas, 1934).

This book is set in a digital version of Bembo, a font designed in 1929 by Monotype and based on a roman typeface cut in 1495 by Francesco Griffo. The display type is Daily News BQ. The paper is Utopia Two Ivory, an acid-free, matte-finish stock certified by the Forest Stewardship Council and meeting the requirements for permanence of the American National Standards Institute. The binding material is Rainbow Sierra, a woven rayon cloth. Printing by Malloy Incorporated. Binding by Dekker Bookbinding. Digital imaging by John and Stephen Stinehour.

Book design and composition by Jonathan Bennett.

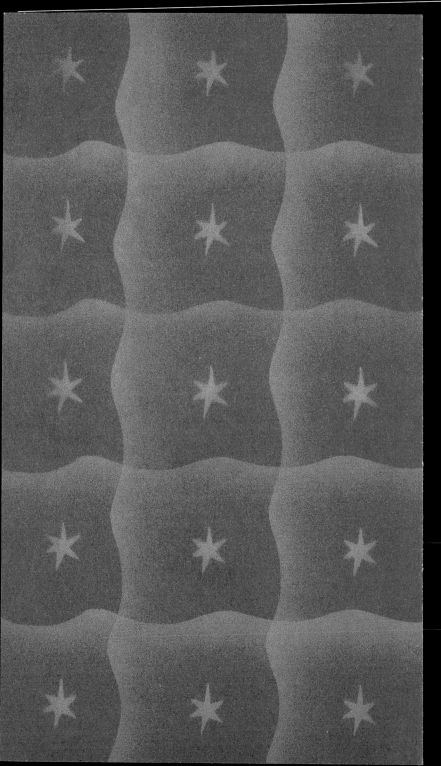